WORRALS
CARRIES ON

Other titles in the Worrals series
available from IndieBooks:

Worrals of the WAAF
Worrals Flies Again

WORRALS CARRIES ON

By W. E. Johns

IndieBooks

Worrals Carries On
By W. E. Johns

ISBN: 978-1-908041-10-4
Originally published in 1942 by the Lutterworth Press
This edition published in 2013 by IndieBooks Limited,
4 Staple Inn, London WC1V 7QH

Illustrations by Matt Kindt (www.mattkindt.com)

© Copyright W. E. Johns (Publications) Ltd
This Edition including design, typesetting and illustrations
© IndieBooks Limited 2013

Printed by Butler Tanner and Dennis
Caxton Road, Frome BA11 1NR

Printed on FSC-certified paper with processes certified to ISO14001

1 3 5 7 9 8 6 4 2

Publisher's Note

Captain W. E. Johns, creator of the legendary air ace 'Biggles', began this series of adventure novels featuring Worrals at the height of the Second World War. Johns had been an RAF fighter pilot himself, and then editor of a children's magazine; so his work combines that vivid experience of flying and combat with an instinctive feel for how to tell a cracking story.

The exploits of Worrals and her side-kick Frecks are not that far from reality. Members of the Women's Auxiliary Air Force were not supposed to serve in combat, or as pilots. In fact, over a hundred women were wartime pilots in the Air Transport Auxiliary, ferrying new and repaired planes to RAF bases, and fifteen were killed doing so. Many members of the WAAF operated behind enemy lines with the Special Operations Executive, mainly as radio operators and couriers, sharing the same dangers with their male counterparts.

If you want to know more about Worrals, or about the courage shown by those who served in the WAAF and ATA, you'll find lots of material at www.indiebooks.co.uk/worrals. Also, you can see some of the planes flown by Worrals and her real-life colleagues at the RAF Musuem sites at Hendon in north London and Cosforth in the West Midlands.

In bringing the Worrals books back into print, we have given them an entirely fresh look and feel, including updating the punctuation to follow modern practice, though the text itself is unchanged. We have commissioned new illustrations from the American artist and writer Matt Kindt, who has previously explored the experience of wartime agents in Europe in his graphic novels, notably the excellent Superspy. We have however preserved an example of the original illustrations, by Stead, in the end-papers.

This new edition is dedicated to those who served in the WAAF and ATA.

For each copy sold we make a donation to the RAF Museum.

CONTENTS

Worrals is Suspicious

Flight Officer Joan Worralson, better known in the W.A.A.F. as 'Worrals', sat on an improvised seat consisting of a plank across two fire buckets, engaged in the anxious occupation of waiting for 'the birds to come home to roost'. That is to say, she was awaiting the return of an offensive patrol of the fighter squadron to which she was attached. Beside her sat her bosom friend and inseparable companion, 'Frecks' Lovell. Not far away a little group of airmen were watching the southern sky with equal interest.

Twelve machines had set out. How many would come back? That was a question in every mind, but nobody ventured to ask it aloud. Such questions are not popular in fighting units.

'Here they come,' murmured Worrals, in a voice that she forced to remain calm.

A cluster of black specks, like midges over

a garden path on a June evening, had appeared against the background of azure blue. The C.O., Squadron-Leader McNavish, D.S.O., appeared at the door of the squadron office, the station adjutant at his elbow. Shading their eyes, they, too, stared at the little group of aircraft, now taking more definite form as they closed the distance between them and the aerodrome.

Worrals began to count. The reached eleven, and stopped. She counted again.

'I make it eleven,' she said in a low voice.

'I can't make it any more,' announced Frecks reluctantly.

'I wonder who's gone?' Worrals' voice was little more than a whisper.

'Don't worry, it won't be Bill,' returned Frecks confidently.

'I didn't say anything about Bill,' protested Worrals. Flying Officer Bill Ashton was her particular pal among the officers of the squadron.

Frecks smiled knowingly. 'I know you didn't say anything,' she answered blandly. 'But that's what you were thinking.'

'Since when have you been clairvoyant?' inquired Worrals sarcastically.

'One doesn't need to be a thought-reader to know who you are most concerned about,' murmured Frecks casually.

Now all this was really forced conversation, a safety valve for strained nerves. Nothing more was said. With a dull rumble the eleven pairs of wheels touched the ground. As the machines swung round towards the hangars, each showed an identification letter, painted in white, on the fuselage, and Worrals breathed a sigh of relief when she saw that Bill's machine was among them.

'It's M that's missing,' she observed.

'That's Leon Joudrier,' returned Frecks. Leon Joudrier was a Belgian pilot recently posted to the squadron.

The whirling propellers slowed down, then stopped. The mechanics ran forward and the pilots climbed stiffly from their cockpits. The C.O. joined them. For a little while they stood in a group, talking, then broke up and moved towards the squadron office to make out their combat reports. Bill Ashton saw Worrals and Frecks, raised his hand in greeting, and walked out of his way to speak to them. He was smiling, but his face was rather pale and drawn with the intense strain of high altitude combat.

'How did it go, Bill?' asked Worrals.

'Warmish,' grinned Bill. 'We reckon we got five Messerschmitts.'

'How many did you get yourself?' inquired Frecks.

Bill held up one finger.

'Nice work.'

'What happened to Joudrier?' asked Worrals.

Bill's smile faded, to be replaced by a puzzled frown.

'Don't know. Nobody seems to know. He was with us when we got to the Channel, but there was a lot of loose cloud about. We went up through it to the sunny-side, and it was then that I first missed Joudrier. There were several Messerschmitts in the offing. I'm afraid he must have bumped into one of them and got the worst of it. Pity! He had the makings of a useful pilot. See you later, kids.'

'Not so much of the kids,' called Frecks indignantly after him.

Bill waved a hand to show that he had heard.

'So Joudrier's gone,' murmured Worrals.

'Well, I'm not going to pretend to shed tears for him. He wasn't a friendly sort of chap.'

'What you mean is, he gave you the frozen shoulder when you spoke to him the other day.'

'I won't deny that,' acknowledged Worrals. 'But I only spoke to him as I would have spoken to any of the other fellows. They're all friendly enough. There was no need for Joudrier to be so churlish. I only hope he didn't think I was tilting my hat at him — but there, what does it matter now? I don't suppose we shall ever see him again. Come on, let's go and get some tea.'

Worrals' assumption that they would not see the Belgian officer again went by the board about two hours later. They had lingered over tea, reported to the adjutant to receive instructions about a machine which was to be taken back to the manufacturers for reconditioning, and were on their way to their quarters when, out of the evening sky, came a Reliant aircraft bearing the letter M on its fuselage.

Worrals pointed.

'Well I'm dashed! Look who's here. Joudrier got back after all. I wonder what sort of tale he'll have to tell? I expect his machine has got shot about. Let's go and look at it.'

Joudrier jumped down, spoke curtly to his mechanics, and then, with hardly a glance at the girls, strode on towards the officers' quarters.

'Bad-tempered brute,' muttered Frecks, as they walked on to the machine.

For a minute or two they looked at it, walking slowly around it looking for bullet holes or other signs of damage. But there was none to be seen.

'Apparently he didn't get into a fight at all,' remarked Worrals, and they were about to turn away from the aircraft when she stopped dead, bending a little to get a better view of something that had attracted her attention. The mechanics were about to wheel the machine in, but she slipped under the wing, removed a small object, and returned to Frecks. Then she stood still, staring at the object which she held in her hand. It was a leaf.

'That's funny,' she said in a puzzled voice, while a frown furrowed her forehead.

'What's funny?' inquired Frecks.

'This leaf.'

'What about it?'

'Don't you recognize it?'

Frecks took the leaf, examined it and smelt it.

'It's geranium,' she observed.

'You're right — more or less. It isn't the common geranium one sees in gardens in this country, though. Smell it again. It's the scented geranium which is used for half the perfumes in the chemists' shops. I happen to have seen it growing.'

'Well, what about it?'

Worrals threw Frecks a peculiar look.

'Enormous quantities are needed for making perfume, so where it is cultivated it is grown in fields,' she declared. 'It only grows in warm countries. I've seen fields and fields of it.'

'Where?'

'In France,' answered Worrals softly. 'It doesn't grow right up in the north, but further south there's plenty of it.'

Frecks frowned.

'What are you driving at?'

'I'm not driving at anything; I'm stating a simple fact,' answered Worrals. 'Work it out for yourself. A machine disappears — one, incidentally, not flown by a British pilot. It comes back long after the others, bringing with it a piece of vegetation which does not grow in this country — at least, not in the open. Doesn't that suggest anything to you?'

'You don't mean. . .you don't think. . .Joudrier landed in France?'

'Can you think of any other way that his aircraft could have picked up that particular leaf?'

Frecks thought for a moment.

'No, not unless Joudrier stuck it where you found it, for some particular purpose.'

Worrals shook her head.

'No, Frecks, that won't do. It's hard to imagine a British aircraft landing in France, but it's still harder to believe that a pilot would decorate his machine with a geranium leaf.'

'Perhaps Joudrier had a forced landing, and got away again?' suggested Frecks.

'That may be the explanation,' agreed Worrals. 'We can soon settle that by checking up on his combat report.'

'Why bother?'

'Because I hate mysteries,' returned Worrals. 'Come on.'

The girls walked over to the squadron office. They were saved the trouble of going in, for they met Bill Ashton coming out. Worrals stopped him.

'I see Joudrier got back after all,' she remarked.

'Yes.'

'What happened to him?'

'He had a spot of engine trouble, and landed at Shoreham to get it put right.'

'You mean — he was there half the afternoon?'

'So he says — why?'

'Nothing,' answered Worrals vaguely. 'Tell me, Bill, would it be possible for a Reliant to get as far as, say, Lyons, and back, without refuelling?'

Bill did some quick mental arithmetic.

'I shouldn't think so,' he decided. 'Speaking from memory, Lyons is a good five hundred miles from here. But that's a funny question to ask. What's on your mind, kid?'

'Don't call me kid,' flared Worrals. 'I'll tell you later. So long.'

The girls walked on, leaving Bill staring after them, a curious expression on his face.

Worrals went straight to her room, got two empty hand lotion bottles, washed them, and then — to Frecks' mystification — went to the hangar that housed Joudrier's machine.

Mechanics were cleaning it down. She spoke to one of them.

'Could you get me a little drop of petrol out of the tank?' she asked sweetly, holding up a bottle.

'I'll get you some out of a can,' offered the aircraftman willingly.

'No, if you don't mind I'd like it from this machine. You see,' — Worrals tried to blush — 'I have a particular regard for Mr Joudrier.'

The mechanic grinned, took the bottle and filled it.

'There you are,' he said.

Worrals thanked him and went to the next hangar. Here she found a flight sergeant.

'Would you mind giving me a drop of petrol to fill my petrol lighter?' she asked, holding up the empty bottle.

'With pleasure,' said the flight sergeant, and filled the bottle.

Worrals returned to her room.

'Say! What on earth do you think you're

playing at?' demanded Frecks. 'Can't you think of something better to do on an evening like this without fooling about filling bottles with petrol? What's the big idea, anyway?'

Worrals did not answer at once. She held up first one bottle to the light, then the other; then she held them both up together and considered the contents. For a full minute she studied them, then set them on the table.

'I'm afraid Leon Joudrier is a fibber,' she remarked quietly.

'What does it matter?' protested Frecks.

'It may matter a lot to some of the boys on this aerodrome,' returned Worrals seriously. 'The question is now, ought I to go and see the C.O.?'

'What's eating you?'

'This,' answered Worrals frankly. 'If I report to the C.O. he may throw me out on my ear. Failing that, he may do something unfortunate, like questioning Joudrier, and thereby warn him that he is suspected. The C.O. doesn't mince matters.'

'Suspect Joudrier? Suspect him of what?'

'I don't know, but something that may not be very nice.'

'If you're not going to tell me what all this is leading up to I'm going to the flicks,' declared Frecks.

'Don't rush me — I'm thinking,' pleaded Worrals. 'Suppose we muster our facts, as they say in books, and see how they look. Joudrier takes off. He comes back two hours after the others, bringing with him — unaware of it — the leaf of a plant that doesn't grow in this country, but grows in France. It was stuck on his wheel. This, I think, indicates that he landed in France. One thing is certain, he didn't only land at Shoreham as he asserted, because I know beyond all shadow of doubt that scented geraniums don't grow on Shoreham aerodrome. Nor, for that matter, do geraniums grow on any other aerodrome that I've ever seen. We may assume, then, that Joudrier landed, but not on an aerodrome, where a geranium — if it tried to grow — would soon be knocked flat.'

Worrals reached for the bottles, but kept them in her hands.

'Do you remember that Heinkel Bill shot down about three weeks ago?' she resumed.

'Of course — we went to look at it.'

'That's right. A petrol expert was there from the Air Ministry, taking a sample of juice from the tank, to check up on the sort of spirit the enemy was using.'

'Yes, I remember perfectly well.'

'Having an inquiring mind I asked him about enemy petrol, and he showed me some. Unlike ours, which has a fair blue tint, the German stuff has a yellowish look about it, due, the inspector said, to some metallic compound which is added to give it extra power.'

'I remember all that.'

Worrals help up one bottle.

'This is our petrol,' she said. 'Note the leaden blue tint. It's quite certain that when Joudrier's machine left this aerodrome today, this is the petrol that would be in his tank.'

'Of course.'

'And this,' went on Worrals in a hard voice, holding up the other bottle, 'is a sample of the petrol which I have just taken from the same tank.'

Frecks caught her breath.

'By gosh! It's yellow,' she whispered.

'Precisely.'

'You knew that?'

'No, but I suspected it would be. If Joudrier has today been within the limits of where the geranium grows, he would need to refuel in order to get back here. It rather looks, doesn't it, as if he had been to the geranium district, and that he was refuelled — with German petrol? The Germans haven't got so much petrol that they leave it lying around, in fields, to be picked up by anybody who happens to want some. If Hun petrol's in Joudrier's tank, and we know it is, then the Huns put it there. And if the Huns put it there, then, indisputably, Joudrier is a friend of there. He says he landed at Shoreham. That, I suspect, is a lie. A man who lies in one matter will lie in another. I'm afraid Joudrier is — '

'A spy!'

'That's a dangerous word,' returned Worrals cautiously, putting the bottles back on the table.

'So what?' queried Frecks.

'I think our next step is to find out if Joudrier did land at Shoreham, and if he did, how long he stayed there. Let's go down to the adjutant's office and get on the telephone.'

Night had fallen, and not a light showed as

the girls made their way to station headquarters. The staff had gone, except the W.A.A.F. telephone operators, who worked in a building some distance away.

'I expect the adjutant's having his dinner,' murmured Frecks. 'What are you going to do — wait for him?'

'I don't think that's necessary,' replied Worrals. She picked up the telephone and called the W.A.A.F. operator. 'Connect me with station headquarters, Shoreham,' she ordered.

A moment later a voice answered.

'This is N Squadron, Westmere,' announced Worrals. 'Please put me through to the duty officer.'

There was a brief delay; then another voice spoke.

'Oh, duty officer,' said Worrals coolly. 'This is Flight Officer Worralson, N Squadron. I have a report here I have to confirm. I believe one of our officers, Flying Officer Joudrier, landed on your aerodrome this afternoon. Would you mind checking that?'

'Just a minute.'

Worrals smiled faintly at Frecks while she

was waiting.

'Yes,' she went on, as the duty officer came back on the line. She listened while he spoke. 'Thanks,' she said, 'much obliged. That's all I wanted to know. Good night.'

She hung up the receiver.

'Well, I wasn't far wrong,' she said quietly to Frecks. 'Joudrier did land at Shoreham, but he didn't fill up there, nor did he report a sticky engine. In fact, he was there for only five minutes, just long enough, I imagine, to establish an alibi in case anyone checked up on his report. Naturally, he wouldn't suppose anyone would ask how long he was there. He stated in his report that he was there all afternoon. Frecks, there's something about this affair that smells distinctly fishy.'

She started as a slight sound came from the door. Both girls looked round quickly. An officer was standing there, just outside the radius of light. It was Leon Joudrier.

2

In Town that Night

Leon Joudrier closed the door and advanced slowly towards the girls until he stood close enough to look down on them.

He was a tall, dark, slim man of about twenty-eight, good-looking in a saturnine way, a characteristic for which a small black moustache and a sallow complexion were largely responsible. Normally, his manner was quick and alert, almost impulsive, but now his movements were slow and deliberate.

'What are you doing here?' he asked in perfect English, but with a pronounced accent.

'I might ask you the same question,' parried Worrals, thinking swiftly.

'I came to see the adjutant.'

'As a matter of fact, so did I,' answered Worrals, truthfully enough.

For a moment, Joudrier regarded her with

thoughtful, brooding eyes. 'I expect the adjutant is in the mess,' he observed. 'I'll go and see. Can I give him a message for you?'

'No, thanks. It wasn't anything important. It can wait until tomorrow.' Worrals turned on her heel. 'Come on, Frecks. Let's get along.'

Joudrier followed them out and strode away in the direction of the officers' mess. The girls watched him go.

'How much did he hear, I wonder?' murmured Frecks.

'That's what I'd like to know,' returned Worrals pensively. 'He must have come in quietly. We don't know how long he'd been standing there. It would be interesting to know what he wanted to see the adjutant about, too.'

'It didn't take him long to say, whatever it was,' answered Frecks quickly. 'He's just come out of the mess. Look! There he goes. Where's he going?'

'It looks as if he's making for the car park,' replied Worrals. 'That means he's leaving camp.'

'How about following him to see where he goes?' suggested Frecks.

Worrals hesitated. 'I don't like spying on

people,' she demurred.

'It looks as if he's not beyond doing a bit of spying,' Frecks pointed out.

'That's true,' agreed Worrals. 'All right, let's go.'

By the time they reached the officers' car park Joudrier was just leaving. The girls scrambled into Worrals' car, and keeping at a safe distance followed him through the main gate.

'He's taking the London road,' remarked Frecks. 'I hope he isn't going to London.'

'Why not?'

'I'd hate to be caught in a blitz. How much petrol have we?'

Worrals glanced at the gauge. 'Enough to get us to London and back. It's under thirty miles each way.'

Nothing more was said for a little while, Worrals concentrating on keeping the red tail light of Joudrier's car in sight.

'It looks as if it's going to be London,' she observed, as the leading car settled down to a steady run on the main road.

Her assumption proved correct, and rather less than an hour later they were moving slowly through the West End. There was little traffic about, so there was no difficulty in keeping the car in sight.

Worrals glanced at her watch. 'Nearly eight o'clock,' she murmured. 'I hope this isn't going to turn out to be a wild goose chase.'

'Ah-huh,' grunted Frecks as Joudrier's car glided into a public car park. 'I guess we're in for a spot of walking.'

It was soon clear that her guess was correct. Joudrier got out of his car, locked it and walked briskly towards Leicester Square. He did not stop there, and the girls nearly lost him in Shaftesbury Avenue, but Frecks' eyes picked him up turning into Compton Street.

'He's making for Soho,' asserted Worrals.

'Soho? That's the foreign quarter, isn't it?'

'Yes. I've been there, to a little restaurant, for lunch once or twice, but I can't say I know the district.'

'What's the name of the street he's turning into now?' asked Frecks, as Joudrier turned sharply into a narrow thoroughfare.

'I haven't the remotest idea,' confessed Worrals. 'We'd better close up a bit or we may lose him. It's dark in these narrow streets without any lights. I hope he isn't going much farther.'

'Funny place for him to come to, isn't it?' queried Frecks.

'Not at all. After all, he's a foreigner,' Worrals pointed out. 'Steady!'

She grabbed Frecks by the arm and pulled her into a shadow as Joudrier stopped and looked up and down the road. Then he disappeared from sight.

'He's gone in somewhere,' said Worrals softly. 'Come on.'

They hurried on to the spot where Joudrier had disappeared, and then stopped, staring at the building that confronted them. Owing to the black-out it was possible to see only one thing clearly, and that was a small illuminated notice, cut in the blind of a door. It announced that the building was the Green Parrot Dance Hall. A smaller notice boasted that dancing was in session, and that the dance hall, being below ground level, was an air raid shelter.

'So what?' inquired Frecks. 'I can't say that I am infatuated with the idea of going into that dive.'

'I'm with you there,' agreed Worrals warmly. 'I don't think it would be advisable to go in, anyway.'

'Why not?'

'Obviously, because Joudrier would see us. He'd know we'd followed him — at least, I can't imagine that he'd be so credulous as to suppose that our arrival here was a coincidence.'

'If we're not going in what are we going to do?'

'There's only one thing we can do, and that's watch for him to come out. Having come all this way we might as well learn as much as possible.'

For perhaps ten minutes the girls stood in an alley entrance near the door of the dance hall, and by the end of that time they were getting bored with their vigil.

'Let's give up and go home,' suggested Frecks.

'Yes, I think that's a sane suggestion,' agreed Worrals, and took a step forward on the pavement preparatory to departing.

At that moment the sirens wailed their sinister warning.

'That's beautiful,' growled Frecks with bitter sarcasm. 'My goodness! What a frightful din.'

'Let's run for it,' cried Worrals. 'If we can get to the car there's just a chance that we may get clear of London before the bombs come down.'

Frecks had no chance to question the wisdom of this suggestion, for at that moment a policeman and an air raid warden appeared. Where they came from neither of the girls saw; not that they gave the matter any thought, for with scant ceremony the police officer bundled them through the entrance of the dance hall.

'Inside, you girls,' he ordered curtly.

'But — ' began Worrals.

The policeman cut her off. 'Take cover,' he said crisply.

'But we're — '

'I don't care who you are. My orders are to clear the streets. Make it snappy now — inside.'

'I think we'd better do as he says,' muttered Frecks anxiously, her eyes upturned to the sky whence now came the flash of bursting shells and the dull thunder of the barrage.

The girls went in, and after descending a short flight of stairs found themselves in the dance hall. The air was blue with tobacco smoke, and discordant with the crash of swing music.

The dancers continued to dance, regardless of the impending raid.

'Phew, what a crowd,' gasped Frecks.

'What an atmosphere,' murmured Worrals. 'You could cut it with a knife.'

'Well, it's a case of any port in a storm,' remarked Frecks tritely, as they took up a position near the wall where the crowd was least pressing.

Worrals surveyed the scene without enthusiasm. There were soldiers, sailors and airmen present, besides civilians, and several W.A.A.F.s, A.T.S.s and other girls in uniform.

'I suppose this sort of thing is all right — for those who like this sort of thing,' mused Frecks.

'I suppose if you happen to be in London without a home it's either this or walking about the gloomy streets,' answered Worrals. 'I don't know which is worse. Hello! Here they come,' she concluded, as the building vibrated to the roar of an explosion not far away.

'It seems to me that we ought to be doing something useful instead of cowering in this rabbit hole,' growled Frecks.

'It may seem that way to you, but the police

wouldn't agree,' replied Worrals.

After that they fell silent, watching the extraordinary scene before them, flinching occasionally as the building shook. Sometimes small pieces of plaster dropped from the ceiling.

'This isn't my idea of a pleasant way of passing an evening,' muttered Frecks. 'What happens if the car gets blitzed?'

'If nothing worse than that happens we shan't have any cause to complain,' rejoined Worrals.

Suddenly she caught Frecks by that arm. 'There he is,' she whispered.

'Who?'

'Joudrier — of course. Over there — look, near that pillar, talking to another man.'

'Frecks looked in the direction indicated, and saw the pilot in conversation with a short, fair-haired, smartly-dressed man of foreign appearance.

'Let's move to a place where he won't be able to see us,' suggested Worrals.

But she was too late. Even as she spoke Joudrier happened to glance in their direction. He stiffened suddenly; his gaze remained fixed, and he half rose in his seat.

'He's spotted us,' muttered Worrals.

Joudrier said something to his companion. He, too, looked in their direction. Then they both rose and moved through the whirling dancers towards the place where the girls stood.

'Here they come,' said Worrals in a low voice. 'I'm afraid this is going to be awkward.'

'I can't see that we've anything to worry about,' returned Frecks indignantly. 'If anybody is in the wrong, he is, not us.'

'He may take a different view of things,' returned Worrals drily. 'Leave the talking to me.'

As it happened the warning was unnecessary, for when Joudrier and his companion were only half way across the hall there was a deafening explosion. The building rocked. A chandelier fell with a crash. Simultaneously, the lights went out.

Worrals caught Frecks by the arm. 'Don't move,' she said tersely. 'Whatever happens we must keep together.

'What about Joudrier?'

'He'll have a job to find us in the dark.'

And there the girls stood for some minutes,

while pandemonium reigned around them. Then the gunfire outside died away, and presently the sirens shrieked 'all clear'.

'Thank goodness,' breathed Worrals fervently.

'For the love of Mike, let's get out of this,' gasped Frecks. 'This darkness is awful.'

A torch cut a wedge of light across the hall. Behind it the girls could just make out the burly figure of a policeman.

'Silence please!' he shouted. Then as the babble of voices died away he continued. 'Nobody may leave the building by the front entrance. There's an unexploded bomb in the road. Form up in line, everybody, and pass quietly out through the back way.'

The buzz of conversation was resumed the moment the policeman finished speaking. The girls found a number of people moving slowly in one direction, so they fell in line and followed.

'I don't like this,' murmured Frecks, as the line left the main hall and entered a narrow corridor.

A man just in front of Worrals held up a lighted petrol lighter. It brought a cheer from most people who were near it, but not from

Worrals, who realized that it would enable Joudrier to see them, and this she was hoping to avoid. As it happened, she saw him first, just in front; he was looking about, obviously in search of her, but Worrals turned her face away, telling Frecks to do the same. Then the petrol lighter expired and the crowd moved on to the rear exit in comparative silence.

As the girls emerged into the open air they discovered that the streets were no longer dark; they were lit up by the lurid glow of a dozen fires.

'How awful,' muttered Frecks, for the moment forgetting about Joudrier.

'There he goes,' whispered Worrals, catching sight of him. Still in the company of the man with whom he had been in the dance hall, the pilot was hurrying down a narrow street.

'So what?' inquired Frecks.

'I'm going to see where they go,' declared Worrals.

'Are you crazy?'

'Possibly, but having come so far I'm going to see the thing through to the end.'

Mixing with pedestrians who were now emerging from the shelters and basements in which they had taken cover, the girls walked on quickly behind the two men whom they could see plainly in the glow cast down by the crimson sky. The chase eventually took them to the river, which rolled on somberly, regardless of the devastation on its banks.

'This is where we shall lose them, I'm afraid,' murmured Worrals, as the men turned into a narrow alley.

The girls had to proceed more warily, for fear of colliding with the men who they could no longer see. Consequently by the time they reached the place where the water lapped dismally against a dilapidated wharf, there was no sign of them — at least, not for some minutes. Then Worrals made out a dinghy being rowed diagonally across the river towards one of those gaunt wooden warehouses that line the southern bank of the Thames below Charing Cross Bridge.

'There they go,' she observed, as the dinghy disappeared into the shadow cast by the tall buildings.

'There's another boat there, if you still feel like following them,' remarked Frecks a trifle sarcastically. She didn't make the suggestion seriously.

But Worrals was too concerned to notice it. 'Where?' she demanded.

'Over there,' Frecks pointed.

Worrals went straight to the boat, a rowing-boat in the last stages of decay.

'Surely you're not thinking of pushing off in that tub?' cried Frecks aghast.

'Why not?'

'Don't ask me,' returned Frecks helplessly. But she followed Worrals into the boat and cast off. 'Of all the crazy stunts I've ever been on, this is about the maddest,' she declared, as Worrals picked up the oars and sent the boat forging through the water.

It took them a good time to reach the far side of the river, and then they were at fault, Worrals resting on her oars, gazing at the dark building that rose up from the very edge of the water. Moving nearer, she saw the dinghy moored to one of the slimy piles of a short, weed draped stairway.

'That's their boat, so they can't be far away,' she observed, as she dipped her oars again. In another minute they had made fast to the stairway, and had climbed out on the mouldering planks.

'Have you any idea of what part of London we're in?' asked Frecks gloomily.

'None whatever,' replied Worrals cheerfully. 'But we're not doing badly. Come on.'

They could find no door, but they discovered a window, the glass of which had been blown out by blast during that night's raid, or a previous one.

'This is the way we go,' whispered Worrals, taking a last survey of the scene.

Near at hand, the ebbing tidal water lapped with sinister monotony. Away to the left were the blazing fires of burning buildings, whence came the confused roar of fire engines speeding through the streets.

Frecks heard the window scrape as Worrals opened it. She followed her, and found herself standing on a boarded floor. Then Worrals' pocket torch cut a beam of light in the darkness. It revealed that the building was what it appeared to be — an abandoned warehouse.

'I should say it's some time since this place was used,' whispered Worrals. 'Note the cobwebs.

Let's go on.'

Brushing aside the cobwebs they advanced with caution, for in spite of their efforts to prevent it the floor creaked alarmingly, and it was in some places so rotten that it seemed not improbable that it would collapse under their weight. Rats scampered in front of them; some were bold enough to watch the intruders from a short distance, their eyes glinting like jewels when the light of the torch caught them. Worrals stopped frequently to listen, but everything was as silent as a tomb.

The girls went on, and after a time came to a rickety staircase leading downwards; another flight led upwards, but Worrals, after a moment's pause, took the steps that led down. They ended in a small open stone-paved area. On the far side was a door. On it, painted on a board, were the words:

THE BONANZO ICE CREAM COMPANY

'Great Scott,' gasped Frecks. 'We've struck an ice cream factory.'

'And there are the tricycles,' whispered

Worrals, pointing to the far side of the yard where, parked in rows, stood a double line of blue and white ice cream tricycles, each bearing the invitation to the public to stop the rider and buy one.

Frecks shivered. 'This is getting eerie,' she breathed nervously. 'I don't want any ice cream tonight, thank you.'

'Neither do I,' mused Worrals. 'What does Joudrier want with them, I wonder?'

Crossing the yard she tried the door. To her surprise it yielded to her pressure. She opened it a little way and listened. From the distance came the echoing murmur of voices in low but excited conversation.

'I think we've run our fox to earth at last,' remarked Worrals softly. 'Let's go and see what's going on.'

With Frecks following close behind, she entered a boarded passageway that lay beyond the door. Other doors occurred on either side of the corridor; one stood ajar; the room beyond was in darkness, but the torch revealed machinery and the accessories of ice cream making and packing — tins, labels and cartons. The voices, however, came from further along the corridor, so the girls went on, Frecks flinching every time a floorboard creaked, as happened not infrequently.

At length the reflection of a light appeared ahead, and Worrals halted, for it was now possible to catch words of the conversation. She judged that at least three men were there, one of them, she could tell by the voice, being Joudrier. But he no longer spoke in English.

'What language are they talking?' breathed Frecks.

'Italian.'

'Can you understand what they're saying?'

'I get a word or two here and there. S-s-h.'

For come minutes the girls stood silent, listening, while the voices rose higher and higher, and it was obvious even to Frecks that an argument was going on. Suddenly there was a brief silence, followed by a shrill cry. It was cut off abruptly by a gunshot which, in the confined space, sounded to Frecks like the clap of doom. Then, only a few paces ahead, a man staggered into the corridor. He seemed to stiffen when he saw the girls standing there. Raising his arms, he uttered a choking cry.

Frecks, who had been bereft of her senses for a moment by the swift sequence of events, suddenly recovered the use of her brain and her limbs. She fled down the passage towards the door. A heavy crash behind her speeded her on her way. She reached the courtyard to find that she was alone.

'Worrals!' she cried in an agony of apprehension. But there was no reply.

For a moment she hesitated, her brain in a whirl, not knowing whether to stay where she was or continue her flight. Then a large dustbin in a corner of the area caught her eye, and she sped towards it like a homing pigeon returning to its loft. She lifted the lid. To her unspeakable relief she saw that the bin was empty — or nearly so. In another moment she had climbed into it and, squatting down, allowed the lid to sink quietly into place, leaving only a narrow crack through which to watch the door.

Breathing heavily, for her heart was thumping uncomfortably, she waited.

3

A Dark Night

Frecks did not have to wait long for the next move in the dangerous game she was playing. There came the sound of swiftly striding footsteps, and her heart sank, for she knew that they were too heavy for Worrals'. Two men appeared. They stopped on the threshold. For a few second neither spoke and in the darkness it was impossible for Frecks to see either of them clearly. Then one muttered something in a low voice. The other answered. There was another brief interval of silence. Then the men went back into the building, closing the door behind them.

Frecks drew in her breath with a gasp of relief. Feeling a little more secure, she found time to think, all her thought being, naturally, of Worrals. Not that it was much use thinking, she reflected bitterly, because she hadn't the remotest idea of what had happened in the passage. She couldn't imagine why Worrals hadn't followed her in her headlong flight.

Some time passed; she couldn't even guess how long, although she knew well enough that in such circumstances the minutes lagged painfully. What to do for the best she did not know — or rather, she couldn't make up her mind. Two or three courses were open to her, she reasoned. She could remain where she was, hoping that Worrals would reappear. She could go and try to find a policeman — not that he would be likely to pay much attention to her improbable story while more pressing matters resulting from the air raid required attention. She could return to, or ring up, the aerodrome, and ask for assistance; or she could go back into the building in a desperate hope of finding Worrals. Of these courses, the last made least appeal. She would have hesitated to enter such a sinister-looking place at any time, but now, feeling certain that a tragedy had been enacted there, she liked the idea still less. Yet, against that, it was the most likely to solve her immediate problem — the whereabouts of Worrals. Such was her apprehension, she felt that to know what had happened to Worrals would be some consolation even for being captured.

At the finish she made up her mind suddenly. Whatever happened, she decided, she must find Worrals. Very slowly, then, she lifted the lid of the bin — not very high, but high enough to enable her to put her arm through the opening in order to grasp the handle on the outside. There was, of course, nothing to hold on the inside. But the operation turned out to be more difficult than she had supposed.

Just what happened she did not know — beyond the fact that she was reaching for the handle — but the lid tilted suddenly. She made a frantic effort to catch it, missed it, and the next instant it had crashed on the paving stones.

Now the lid of a dustbin, dropped on hard stone, makes a noise at any time. But in the silence of the night, and in the small enclosed area with high walls on all sides, the noise was indescribable. To Frecks, who instinctively shrank back into the bin with her hands over her ears, the noise seemed to go on for minutes before it died away. There was nothing she could do except sit where she was and hope for the best.

Strangely enough, nothing happened.

Nobody came to the door. It seemed incredible that such a pandemonium had not been heard by the men in the building, yet all remained silent. A minute passed, and another, and Frecks began to recover her shattered composure. She looked about her, surveying the wooden walls that hemmed her in; they were pitted with innumerable windows, in most of which the glass was broken, but all were in darkness so told her nothing. In fact, all the survey told her was that she would learn nothing from the outside of the warehouse.

Getting out of the bin she automatically dusted her clothes before walking quietly to the door. She turned the handle. The door remained closed. That it might be locked was a possibility that had not occurred to her, no doubt because it had been open in the first place; now, the discovery gave her a rude shock.

For a little while she stood still, thinking fast, but as the shock passed she went swiftly to the nearest window. The glass, like the rest, had been shattered, so there was no difficulty about slipping the catch. Before attempting to open the window she listened; but all remained silent, so she raised the sash, flinching a little at the noise it made, and then crept inside. It was in utter darkness. She groped her way to the corridor, but there was no longer any glow from the far end, and as she had no torch she was at a loss to know how to proceed.

How long she stood there in the pitch blackness she did not know. She lost all count of time. But after a while, encouraged by the silence that remained unbroken, she went on, groping along the wall, taking a step at a time and testing each one before moving her weight forward. In this way she had taken some twenty paces when a sound brought her to an abrupt halt. It was the faint creak of a loose board, nothing more; but it came from a short distance away, and as she had been standing still at the time she knew that she was not responsible for it. In an instant she had pressed herself as flat as possible against the wall, every nerve tense, listening. But the noise was not repeated. Instead, there came an even more alarming sound. It was a soft, measured breathing. This settled any doubt that may have lingered in her mind. She knew that she was not alone in the corridor.

If, before, her nerves had been strained to breaking point, they now threatened to snap, and it was only by a tremendous effort of will that she suppressed a scream. Her lips went dry with horror as she stared into the inky darkness. She could see nothing, but she could hear, and the sound she heard was the faint swish of clothing, no louder than the rustle of an autumn leaf. To her intense satisfaction the sound seemed to be receding. Then came silence, utter and complete. Still she dare not move.

Seconds passed. Then, the deathly hush was shattered by a noise so violent that she shrank back, flinching. It was almost like a physical blow, although she knew well enough what had made it. It was the clatter of the ashbin lid. Obviously, someone had touched it. But who? She was soon to know. Clear and crisp, some distance away, came a voice.

'Frecks, where are you?' it said.

Frecks nearly fainted with relief. For the voice was Worrals'.

'Here I am,' she cried shrilly, and started retracing her steps towards the window by which she had entered. But she had not got far when a man's voice shouted:

'Hi! Come here.'

Frecks did not obey. She sped on down the corridor, and made a blind rush for the window. Reaching it, she saw the vague silhouette of Worrals standing outside.

'Look out!' she shouted, as she fell through the window. 'There's a man behind me.'

'Come on,' snapped Worrals. 'Run for it.'

'Run where?' gasped Frecks, who was in a daze.

'The boat. I can't find any other way out,' said Worrals crisply.

Together they sped up the staircase by which they had descended to the yard. Behind them came their pursuer. They could not see him, but they could hear him. There was no longer any question of moving quietly. Their feet clattered on the boards. Rats scuttled, squealing with fright.

Worrals reached the window first, and slipped through; but Frecks was only half way over the sill when a strong hand closed on her shoulder and held her.

'Not so fast young lady, not so fast,' said a firm voice.

Frecks shouted for help, struggling violently; but for all her efforts she could not free herself. The next thing she knew was that Worrals had come back, and was speaking in furious tones to her captor.

'Let go of my friend at once,' she ordered

crisply. 'What do you think you're doing?'

'That's what I'm going to ask you,' came the curt answer. 'I would advise you to make less noise.'

'Nobody asked for your advice,' snapped Frecks, shaking herself free.

'You may be glad to take it,' was the answer. 'Come with me.'

'I shall do nothing of the sort.'

The man sighed. There was a sharp metallic click. Before Frecks could fully realize what was happening the click had been repeated. Ice cold bands encircled her wrists.

'Worrals,' she nearly wept, 'he's put handcuffs on me.'

'And on me,' returned Worrals dully.

'Come this way,' ordered the man, and switching on a powerful torch walked back the way they had come. The girls followed — they had no choice in the matter.

After traversing numerous passages the man opened an outside door and they found themselves in a narrow street. The man walked on, took a turning, turned again, and pulled up by a motor car parked at the kerb.

'Get in,' he ordered.

'Where are you going to take us?' demanded Worrals.

'You'll see.'

'I insist that you tell us. If you don't, I'll. . .'

The man laughed quietly.

'You're in no case to insist on anything,' he pointed out with disconcerting truth. 'But if you must know, we're going to police headquarters.'

Worrals reeled. For a moment she seemed to choke for words.

'*Where* did you say?'

'Scotland Yard. Come on, don't talk so much.'

'Do you mean you're a policeman?' cried Worrals incredulously.

'Well, not exactly; but something like it.'

'Why the dickens didn't you say so?' gasped Worrals indignantly. 'You'd have saved us, and yourself, a lot of trouble.'

By this time they were all in the car, the girls in the back seat. Then, for the first time, the man turned the light of his torch on them. It seemed that it was his turn to be surprised.

'What's this?' he asked sharply. 'Are those W.A.A.F. uniforms?'

'They are,' retorted Worrals.

'What's the idea?'

'We happen to be officers of the W.A.A.F.'

The man stroked his chin in obvious perplexity.

'Somehow, those uniforms don't fit in with that building,' he said. 'What were you doing there?'

Worrals was in no mood to dissemble.

'If you want to know, we were spy hunting,' she announced.

'Is that so?' murmured the man slowly. 'This gets funnier and funnier.'

'It may seem funny to you, but I'm not amused,' put in Frecks bluntly.

The man laughed aloud, and leaning over removed the handcuffs.

'I think it's time we had a little talk,' he said cheerfully. And with that he drove off.

Where they went Worrals did not know, and she only got her bearings when they crossed over Westminster Bridge. As the car sped past Scotland Yard she cried:

'Here, I thought you said you were going to police headquarters?'

'That was my original intention, but they don't make very good coffee there,' was the calm answer. 'I know a better place.'

This turned out to be no idle boast. The car ran on into Jermyn Street and stopped outside what turned out to be a small but excellent restaurant. The head waiter hurried forward.

'Table for three, Joseph,' ordered the girls' escort, with easy familiarity, and they were soon snugly ensconced in a quiet corner.

'What would you like? . . . Tea. . .or coffee and sandwiches?'

Frecks unfroze.

'Coffee and sandwiches sounds pretty good to me,' she decided, for the first time able to see the face of their new acquaintance.

He turned out to be a good-looking, keen-faced young man of about twenty-five or twenty-six, with steady grey eyes and a firm chin. It was the type of face one instinctively trusts.

'Now,' he resumed, when the refreshments had been put on the table, 'I want you to tell me just what you were doing in the place where I found you.'

'How do we know you are what you pretend

to be?' inquired Worrals cautiously.

The man smiled.

'Not taking any chances, I see,' he remarked with gentle sarcasm, taking a small leather wallet from his pocket. He opened it and passed it to Worrals.

Looking over her shoulder Frecks saw that the wallet carried a card stamped with the Home Office stamp. It required all whom it might concern to render the bearer all possible assistance.

'I gather you're in the Intelligence Service?' observed Worrals, passing back the wallet. 'Have you by any chance got a name?'

'You can call me Major Grey,' was the answer, spoken softly. 'Now, if you don't mind, I'll ask the questions. Just who are you?'

There was something in the way the question was asked that brooked no denial. Worrals complied, and gave the officer their names, ranks and station.

'What were you doing in that building?'

'The story doesn't begin there,' Worrals pointed out.

'Then start where it does begin, and omit

nothing. It may be important.'

Forthwith, Worrals, glad to unburden herself of what she felt had become a responsibility, told the story of their adventures, beginning with the discovery of the geranium leaf on the landing gear of Joudrier's aircraft.

The Intelligence officer heard her out without once interrupting.

'Well,' he said slowly as Worrals concluded, 'I must say you girls have got some pluck — more pluck, perhaps, than discretion. Do you realize that you've been intruding in what is acknowledged to be the most dangerous side of war? Believe me, had the men in that building known that you were there, and were watching them, they would have — er — disposed of you without the slightest compunction. The river was handy, and the police are overworked, so no one would ever have known what had become of you.'

'Oh I realize all that,' agreed Worrals. 'What about it? Quite a lot of people are risking their lives in this war. Is there any reason why we should be exceptions?'

Major Gray lit a cigarette.

'Well, no, I suppose not, if you put it like

that.'

'What were you doing in that building, anyway?' inquired Worrals.

'The same thing as you, only I approached from a different angle. I was watching another man, and my quest took me there. As a matter of fact I was in an ice cream refrigerator when the shooting took place. I suppose you know that a man was shot there tonight?'

Frecks stared, aghast.

'Not Joudrier?' queried Worrals quickly.

'No.'

'Who?'

'I'm sorry, I can't tell you.'

'Did you know about Joudrier?'

'No, but I fancy I can see how he fits into the party.'

'Where is he now?'

'He left. They all left, by the same route they came — the river.'

'You mean — they had already left when I came back in?' asked Frecks.

'That's right. I was just about to leave myself when I heard someone slinking down that passage. Of course, I didn't know you girls were in the building till I heard your voices, and that, I must admit, puzzled me not a little. I decided to take a closer look at you.'

'Why didn't you arrest this gang, and have done with it?' questioned Worrals, ever practical.

Major Gray smiled wanly.

'Unfortunately it isn't as easy as all that. We don't work that way in my business. These men you saw tonight are only operatives. Before we strike, we try to find out how far the ramifications of the organization extend, so that we can locate the leaders, both at home and abroad.'

'And what do you advise us to do now? Shall we tell our C.O. what has happened?'

'Certainly not. The fewer people who know about this the better. My advice is, go back to your station and carry on as usual; but you could do me a service by keeping an eye on this man Joudrier and letting me know his movements. I can't be in half a dozen places at once; and not being an air pilot I couldn't follow the fellow into the air. You might be able to do that.'

'We'll have a jolly good shot at it,' declared Worrals eagerly.

Major Gray took a card from his pocket and

passed it to her.

'That's my address,' he said. 'If I am not at home it will be quite safe to leave a message with Captain White, my assistant. What you have already told me is intensely interesting — not to say useful. It's too early to say for certain, but it rather looks as if this man Joudrier might be the connecting link between enemy operatives in this country and overseas. The most important factor at the moment is, does he know you suspect him — that you have been watching him?'

Worrals shook her head.

'I don't know. He may have heard what I said in the squadron office, or he may not. He certainly saw us in the dance hall, and he would certainly regard that as a queer coincidence. He didn't see us in the warehouse; nor did he know that we followed him there.'

'I see. Well, do nothing to arouse his suspicions. Now I must be getting along.'

'So must we,' asserted Worrals. 'Great Scott! It's nearly midnight. We shall get rapped over the knuckles for being out without a late pass.'

That ended the debate. The girls shook hands with their new friend, and finding the car as they had left it were soon on their way back to the aerodrome. Naturally, they had plenty to talk about, and by the time they were approaching the station they had discussed the affair from every angle. The last thing that occurred to either of them was that the night's adventures were not over.'

They had left the main highway, and were cruising slowly down the secondary road that led to the aerodrome, when Worrals noticed a red tail light in front of them; and she was soon able to make out that it was stationary.

'It looks as though somebody has had a breakdown,' she remarked casually.

A moment later a figure appeared in the road, with arms raised.

'Wants a lift,' added Worrals, applying the brake. 'Well, we've plenty of room.'

She brought the car to a standstill and pushed open the door on her side.

'What's the matter?' she asked cheerfully. 'Having some trouble?'

'Yes,' answered the man slowly. 'There is trouble.'

The man stepped nearer. But Worrals did not

need to look at his face to know who had stopped them. She had recognized the voice.

'Why, if it isn't Monsieur Joudrier,' she said evenly, forcing her voice to remain calm. 'Do you want a lift?'

'No, thanks,' answered Joudrier. 'I would rather not leave my car here. I have a flat tyre. There is a spare wheel, but I have no jack. Would you mind lending me yours?'

Now Worrals had a jack, but it was in the back of the car. To get it meant getting out. It was after midnight, and the road was deserted. For a fleeting instant she hesitated.

'Certainly you can have mine,' she said. 'If you like I'll help you to change the wheel.'

To Frecks she whispered:

'Stay where you are, but get in the driving seat.'

Then she stepped out on the road.

4

Flying Blind

As Worrals went to the back of the car to get out the jack her easy manner gave no indication of her nervous tension, for she felt sure that Joudrier, either by word or deed, would reveal that he knew he had been followed — if, in fact, he suspected it. And Worrals thought it was worth taking a chance to find out how much he knew. So she took out the jack and walked over to where Joudrier was standing by his car, watching her.

'Which tyre is flat?' she asked calmly, deliberately forcing the issue, for in her heart she had a strong suspicion that there was nothing wrong with Joudrier's car.

'The back one — this side,' answered Joudrier.

To her surprise, Worrals found that the tyre was really flat, although she did not overlook that the pilot could have let the air out of it through the valve.

'Well, here you are, go ahead,' she invited, standing the jack on the road. She had no intention of doing the work for him.

Joudrier rested his hand on the instrument, but made no attempt to employ it. There was a rather embarrassing silence for a moment or two; then he spoke.

'There's something I want to ask you,' he said abruptly.

'Yes?' queried Worrals.

'Are you a member of the Green Parrot Club?'

'Certainly not,' answered Worrals frankly, knowing that it was useless to deny that they had been there. 'As a matter of fact,' she continued, 'I've never been there in my life until tonight.'

'What made you go there?'

So that was it, thought Worrals swiftly. Joudrier was worried because he knew she and Frecks had seen him there. He was trying to find out what had taken them there.

'I might ask you the same question,' she countered.

Joudrier thought for a moment, considering her with brooding eyes.

'A man can go where it is not always safe for a girl to go. I'd keep clear of that place if I were you.'

'I don't suppose I shall ever go there again,' returned Worrals truthfully. 'I shouldn't have gone there tonight of my own free will.'

'What do you mean?' asked Joudrier sharply.

'I was pushed in by a policeman,' explained Worrals. 'We were near the place when the sirens went and we were ordered to take shelter. That's how we happened to be there.'

'I see,' answered Joudrier slowly.

'What about getting on with the wheel?' prompted Worrals. 'We can't stand here talking all night. By the way, have you got a late pass?'

'Yes, that's why I wanted to see the adjutant.'

Footsteps approached, and glancing up Worrals saw an airman striding down the road carrying a kit bag.

'I expect this boy's going to the camp,' she observed. 'I'll give him a lift. You can bring the jack along with you and give it back to me in the morning.'

She had decided that no useful purpose was to be served by prolonging the conversation.

'What's the hurry?' asked Joudrier quickly.

'Nothing, except that I haven't a late pass,' replied Worrals. Then, without giving Joudrier an opportunity to protest, she turned to the airman who was now level with them, and offered him a lift to the aerodrome — if that was his destination.

The airman, who turned out to be a corporal, accepted with alacrity so, leaving Joudrier still standing by his car watching her reflectively, she got into her seat, and with the airman aboard proceeded on her way.

'That turned out to be a pointless conversation,' remarked Frecks.

Worrals agreed.

'I still think he waited for us deliberately,' she remarked. 'He's a bit worried. He was anxious to find out what we were doing at the Green Parrot, but he daren't press his questions too hard for fear of giving himself away.'

'It looks as if he still doesn't know how much we know.'

'Exactly,' murmured Worrals. 'His own guilty conscience makes him suspicious — it's bound to. Unless he heard me ring up Beach Bay to check his report, all he knows for certain is that we turned up tonight at the Green Parrot. That's got him guessing.'

As Worrals finished speaking she turned in to the aerodrome entrance, where she was challenged and stopped by the sentry on duty. Getting out to 'report in', she was mildly surprised to see the whole guard lined up outside the guardhouse. A moment later she saw the reason. The orderly officer was there. She breathed a sigh of relief when she noticed it was Bill Ashton. The corporal to whom they had given the lift thanked them and disappeared into the building. Bill finished inspecting the guard and then came over to the girls.

'Where's your pass,' he inquired curtly. 'Why, it's you, Worrals,' he went on quickly. 'What on earth are you doing out at this hour? Anybody in the car?'

'Only Frecks.'

'Got a late pass?'

'No.'

'What's the idea — looking for trouble? You know what the Old Man is like about you girls staying out late.'

'I suppose you'll have to report us?'

'I'm afraid I must. Duty is duty. This looks like confining you to camp for fourteen days — unless you've got a pretty good explanation.'

'We were caught in a blitz, in London, and had to take cover.'

'In *London*? Are you crazy? You know perfectly well that officers aren't allowed in London without a special pass. If you tell the C.O. you've been to London you'll get it in the neck. An officer was court-martialled last week for the same thing.'

Worrals thought fast. It was going to be difficult to tell the C.O. the truth after Major Gray had expressly asked her to say nothing. On the other hand, to be confined to camp would mean that she would be unable to carry out his request and keep Joudrier under observation.

'Bill,' she said softly, 'I'm in a jam.'

'You're telling me,' murmured Bill sarcastically.

'Worrals made up her mind to tell him the facts. He could be trusted, and it would relieve her mind to know that a reliable man was *au fait* with the situation. He had proved himself to be a useful comrade in their last spy quest, and she owed frankness to him on that account.

'Have you finished your round?' she inquired.

'Yes — just.'

'Then can we go somewhere and talk? I've something very important to tell you.'

Bill's manner changed at the serious tone of Worrals' voice.

'Okay,' he agreed. 'Can't we stay here?'

'No.'

'Why not?'

'Because in a few minutes an officer will be coming in and I don't want him to see me talking to you.'

'Who is it?'

'Joudrier.'

'What's the idea?'

'Get in the car and I'll move on; then I'll tell you.'

Bill got in, and Worrals drove on to a quiet corner near the girls' quarters. Then she stopped the engine, extinguished the lights, and in a low voice took Bill into her confidence, telling him the whole story.

He listened without a word until she had finished.

'That's all,' concluded Worrals when she came

to the end.

'All! Suffering mike! About enough, too,' muttered Bill. 'All the same, it sounds to me more like a beginning. You kids must be stark raving mad to get yourselves mixed up in a thing like this.'

'Well, there it is,' answered Worrals helplessly. 'We didn't go out of our way to get involved. The geranium leaf started it, and that, I own freely, was sheer curiosity. But having started we had to go on.'

'And what are you going to do now?'

'Nothing — except of course keep an eye on Joudrier, as Major Gray asked us. If we're confined to camp we shan't be able to do that, so you'll have to help us.'

'How?'

'By watching Joudrier in the air when you're on ops. We shouldn't be able to do that anyway. One of the reasons I've told you all this is in the hope that you will watch Joudrier when you're over France. You can also help us by forgetting that we came in late.'

'That's all wrong, Worrals. You know that as well as I do.'

'In a case like this I don't agree,' protested Worrals. 'We're not trying to serve our own ends. What we have done, and what we are doing now, is in the best interests of the country. We have no ulterior motive. The Higher Command, if they knew the facts, would agree. After all, we boast that we are superior to the Nazis because we are encouraged to use our own initiative. This is a case in point.'

'Worrals,' said Bill sadly, 'when the war's over you'd better be a barrister. You'd make a judge believe that black is white. All right — I'll do it. Your names won't appear in my report, but if there's a row, and it's found out, you'll have to —'

'I'll come and whisper nice things to you through the prison bars,' promised Worrals. 'But seriously, Bill, I'm sure we're doing the right thing.'

'Maybe you're right,' agreed Bill. 'But it's time you were in bed. I'll put the car away for you if you like. What are you doing tomorrow?'

'I've got to take an old Reliant to the aircraft park at Ragworth, and bring a new one back.'

Bill glanced at the sky.

'You look like having a dirty trip. The clouds

are coming down, and there's rain about.'

'What are you doing tomorrow?' asked Worrals.

'Nothing in particular. I get the day off after doing orderly dog, so unless Jerry comes over I shall probably stand easy. I may test my machine.'

Worrals and Frecks got out of the car.

'See you later, Bill,' Worrals said softly.

'So long, kids,' murmured Bill, pressing the starter.

'Kid yourself,' snapped Frecks.

Bill laughed quietly as the car slid away into the darkness.

Dawn proved Bill's prophesy, concerning the weather, correct. Leaden clouds trailed sluggishly across the sky, dripping the clammy moisture known in the north as a Scotch mist, and in the south as a Dartmoor drizzle. Visibility was practically zero. From the meteorological office Worrals learned that the murk which clung to the ground was from three to four thousand feet thick. She walked over to the squadron office, and there needed little persuasion to postpone her trip to the aircraft park until the weather cleared.

Not until late afternoon did it show signs of lifting, and even then it was far from fair. Had she not been bored, Worrals would have abandoned delivery of the old machine until the following day, for there was no urgency about it; but with her brain working overtime on the Joudrier problem she felt the need for action. One or two machines had been brought out, and the engines were being run up before being tested in the air; but of Joudrier there was no sign. After gazing at the sky for some time she found Frecks, who was working on a mess roster, and told her that she had decided to make the flight to Ragworth.

'I think it's a good opportunity,' she said. 'Joudrier is probably in the officers' mess. It would be better to get the job done now than have to go when he is on the prowl. We don't want to miss anything. Are you coming with me?'

'Sure,' declared Frecks. 'I'm nearly through. I can finish the job when I come back.'

Putting only raincoats over their uniforms, for it was not cold, the girls made their way to the hangar that housed the aircraft due for repair, and ordered it to be brought out. In five minutes it was ready for take-off, and Worrals was taxiing into position when Frecks spoke.

'I thought you said Joudrier was in the mess,' she said sharply.

'I couldn't think of anywhere else he could be.'

'Well, he's not in the mess now. He's standing over there by his machine. It's just been brought out. It looks as if he's going to do a spot of testing.'

'That's a nuisance,' muttered Worrals. 'Still, we can't do anything about it now. I've booked out, and I can't go back without a good excuse. I'll tell you what,' she went on quickly. 'We'll get up topsides and wait for him to come through the mist. He won't know we're in the air. We ought to be able to see which way he goes. The direction he takes might tell us something.'

'That's an idea,' agreed Frecks.

The engine roared, and the Reliant sped across the soaking turf into the air. For a few seconds Worrals held its nose down for speed, and then with her eyes on the instruments zoomed up into the mist. The scene below faded, and the engine changed its note as the airscrew bit into the swirling mist. A minute of discomfort, and the Reliant burst out into clear sunshine. Overhead, the canopy of heaven was azure blue, clear and serene, with the sun well down in the west; below, a slowly moving mass of clouds came rolling over the edge of the world in endless procession, to pass on and vanish for all time into the distance.

For a little while, for the sheer joy of it, Worrals roared through the solitude, the aircraft skimming the cloud tops like a dolphin in a silver sea while its shadow, huge and distorted, kept it company. Then she drew the control column back and climbed steeply towards the sun.

'If we sit up in the sun it's unlikely that he'll notice us,' she told Frecks, knowing that unless he suspects danger a pilot avoids looking directly into the eye of the sun on account of its dazzling effect.

Not until the altimeter registered ten thousand feet did she put the machine on an even keel; then she began cruising in wide circles, watching the place where Joudrier should appear. Presently a machine came through the mist. Worrals roared after it, but seeing that it bore the marking of a Flight Commander, which meant that the pilot could not be Joudrier, she turned back to her old position. Minutes passed, and nothing happened.

'If he's coming I wish he'd come,' muttered Frecks.

'So do I,' declared Worrals. 'We can't footle about here indefinitely.'

'Look! Who's that — way down to the south?' Frecks spoke tersely.

Worrals turned in the direction indicated and saw a sleek shape stealing southward. Getting into a position between it and the sun she sped after it and, having the advantage of height, rapidly overtook it. Her keen eyes soon made out a large white letter M painted on the side of the fuselage.

'That's our man,' she announced. 'He couldn't have come straight up through the cloud or we should have seen him at once. He must have sat in the soup until he was well clear of the aerodrome.'

'Practising blind flying,' suggested Frecks drily.

'Don't you believe it,' returned Worrals. 'I should say he didn't want to be spotted.'

'What are you going to do — follow him?'

'I don't know what to do, and that's a fact,' answered Worrals. 'I feel we ought to find out where he's going, and what he's doing; on the other hand, this aircraft has got to be delivered to Ragworth and I don't want to get too far off my course. It's getting late, and if the clouds drop again we may have a sticky time trying to find the aerodrome.'

'Suppose we follow him a little way?' suggested Frecks. 'He may be doing a genuine test, in which case he'll soon turn back. If he does we can go on to Ragworth.'

'Yes, we could do that,' agreed Worrals, without taking her eyes off the objective machine.

Some minutes passed before either of them spoke again. Then Worrals said: 'I daren't go much further. We must be getting near the coast. It's ideal weather for enemy aircraft to snoop about, and we should look a pair of fools if we bumped into a Hun.'

'What would you do if we did?' queried Frecks.

'Bolt,' replied Worrals promptly. 'There'd be a nice old row if we got this machine shot up.

They'd never let us fly again.'

Worrals stared down at the clouds.

'I say, take a look at the way those cloud tops are being torn off,' she muttered. 'That can only mean one thing — wind. I thought we were in still air, but apparently we're not. We must be over the Channel. I'm going to turn.'

'Just a minute,' cried Frecks shrilly. 'There's another machine ahead — right against Joudrier.'

Worrals looked. And as her eyes focused on the newcomer she felt her heartstrings tighten.

'It's a Messerschmitt 109,' she said harshly.

'That's what I thought,' declared Frecks. 'In that case why doesn't it attack Joudrier?'

Even as she spoke a red signal flare dropped from the British aircraft. And then, to her utter amazement, the Messerschmitt turned away.

'The flare was a signal,' said Worrals crisply. 'Those two machines must have an arrangement.'

'Say! Did you see that?' shouted Frecks excitedly.

Worrals had seen it. A black and white streamer had dropped from Joudrier's Reliant and plunged down into the billowing clouds that concealed the earth.

'That's a message bag,' she declared. 'What's the idea, I wonder, dropping a message there? Had it been over France. . .'

Frecks broke in with a cry of dismay. 'That Hun has seen us — he's turned towards us. Come on! Let's get out of this.'

Worrals needed no second invitation, for she, too, had seen the Messerschmitt's sudden swerve in their direction. It was still some distance away, but too close for comfort.

In a flash Worrals had whirled the Reliant round and was heading back over her course with the nose of the machine held down at a steep angle. The roar of the engine rose to a bellow, and the air howled and screamed as it clutched in vain at the streamlined fuselage. The cloud seemed to float up to meet them. Yet with all that, the Messerschmitt, a single-seater, closed the distance between them. Frecks, stiff with horror, could only stare at it, for she had no gun; as the machine had only been going to the repair depot the mobile gun had been taken off before the flight.

'Faster!' she screamed. 'He's catching us.'

Worrals nearly stood the Reliant on its nose.

In the clouds she knew she would be comparatively safe, and because she felt sure that she could beat the enemy aircraft to it she was not unduly perturbed.

'Take it easy,' she told Frecks. 'We're nearly there.'

And at that moment the engine cut out dead. An instant later it came on again, but only for a second. The sound ended in a violent backfire.

The airscrew stopped.

'What's happened?' yelled Frecks.

'The engine has died on us — sounds like ignition trouble,' answered Worrals, as the aircraft sank into the clammy surface of the cloud.

'Phew, that was close,' muttered Frecks. 'That Hun was right on our tail. Another jiffy and he would have been within range.'

Worrals did not answer immediately. She was looking at the altimeter. It registered 6,000 feet, but she knew that they were lower than that because in a power dive the needle of the instrument tends to lag. That is to say, it does not entirely keep pace with the dive.

Having brought the machine to a steady glide she spoke.

'Frecks,' she said calmly, 'you realize what's likely to happen?'

'I certainly do,' answered Frecks in a funny voice.

'Everything depends on what we find underneath us. If there's a decent-sized field handy when we come out of this soup I may be able to get into it the right side up; if there isn't, I'm afraid something will get bent.'

Frecks said nothing. There was nothing to say. She understood the situation as well as Worrals. Without the engine the aircraft must go on down, whatever lay below.

Worrals held the machine steady. The air moaned and sighed over the wings. The aircraft was down to a thousand feet now, and still there was no sign of the fog thinning.

'If this stuff is resting on the floor I'm afraid it's going to be just too bad,' she announced in an ominously calm voice.

Frecks did not answer.

The machine continued to nose downward into the white vapour. Worrals, flying blind, occasionally peering below, moistened her lips. The best she could hope for was that they would not collide head on with a tree or a building. At four hundred feet there was still no sign of the ground. Relentlessly the altimeter needle dropped back — 300 — 200 — 100.

Worrals drew a deep breath. She knew that at any moment now they might hit the ground, for her altimeter was set at zero and she had no means of knowing the height above sea level of the ground below. Suddenly the air grew brighter.

Simultaneously a dark shadow loomed up below. In a flash Worrals had flattened out, and in the dead silence the machine glided on, losing speed and sinking slowly. Everything depended now on what lay ahead. Whatever it happened to be there was nothing she could do about it. The machine sank bodily. The tail dropped. The wheels bumped, bumped again on rough ploughed earth, and the aircraft ran slowly to a standstill. A short distance ahead a dark wall rose up, and peering at it Worrals made out the edge of a wood.

She turned to Frecks. 'If we live to be a hundred we shan't have a luckier break than that,' she announced in a strained voice. 'We struck an open field. Another thirty yards and we should have been into a wood.'

'If you hadn't kept your head we should have been in a mess anyway,' declared Frecks. 'What a beast of a day.'

Worrals opened the hood, stood up and peered into the mist that surrounded them. 'You're right,' she agreed. 'I can't see a thing except fog.'

'What are we going to do?'

'Dismount and find out where we are. Then I

shall have to find a telephone to let the adjutant know what's happened. I'm afraid thi isn't going to make us popular with the C.O.'

They climbed down, and leaving the machine as it stood set off across the field. They came to a low hedge and climbed over it into a lane.

'Which way?' asked Frecks, looking up and down.

'Either way,' returned Worrals. 'It's all the same.'

They walked on for a little way and presently reached a dilapidated signpost leaning over at a drunken angle.

'That's funny,' murmured Frecks. 'I thought all signposts had been taken away.'

Worrals did not answer. With a puzzled frown she was reading the name on the post. It was St Vance. 'I never heard of that place,' she said slowly.

Before Frecks could reply a girl appeared. She wore a shawl over her head and shoulders and carried a basket on her arm.

'Excuse me, but would you please tell us where we are?' inquired Frecks politely.

The girl raised her eyebrows. A look of fear

flashed into her eyes and she glanced swiftly up and down the road. '*Pardon*,Mademoiselle?'

'She must be French,' remarked Frecks casually. 'Perhaps she's a refugee.'

Worrals did not answer her. Her face was pale as she addressed the girl in French. 'Are we in — France?' she asked in a strangled voice.

The girl nodded. '*Oui, M'selle. C'est la France*,' she answered, and strode on into the fog.

The sound of her footsteps died away to silence. The girls looked at each other. Their faces were white. Neither spoke.

5

In France

Frecks was the first to speak.

'We're in France,' she said in a dazed voice.

'Sorry, Frecks,' answered Worrals. 'It was my fault. And I call myself a pilot,' she went on bitterly. 'There must have been a fifty mile an hour wind at the height we were flying.'

'You weren't to know it.'

'I should have made allowance for the possibility.'

'The met. officer must have known. Didn't he warn you?'

'I didn't consult him,' confessed Worrals.

'Joudrier did, evidently.'

'What makes you think that?'

'Because he knew just where to drop that message bag. At any rate he must have known he was over France. We thought we were still over England.'

'Yes, that's true. No doubt he had an assignation with that Messerschmitt. But there, it's no use thinking about that now.'

'We certainly are in a spot,' muttered Frecks. 'The question is, what are we going to do about it?'

'We've one chance, and it's a pretty slim one,' opined Worrals. 'And that is, go back to the machine and try to put the engine right.'

'Do you think you can?'

Worrals shrugged her shoulders.

'I don't know until I've had a look at it. There's just a chance, a poor one I must admit, but still, a chance. The fog is now in our favour, otherwise the machine would have been seen. If the fog lifts before dark we shall have to set fire to the aircraft. That, really, is our first duty, to prevent it from falling into the hands of the enemy.'

'It's getting dark now', Frecks pointed out. 'With luck it should be several hours before we are discovered, and in that time we might find out what's wrong with the engine and put it right.'

'If the fog thins we shan't be able to use a light, and the idea of working on an engine in the dark doesn't exactly fill me with enthusiasm. Still, we can only try. Let's get back to the machine for a start.'

Without further discussion the girls went back into the field and struck off into the mist. If anything, it was worse. Its colour was now dark grey, this being due, as Frecks had pointed out, to the approach of night. They walked for some time in silence, pausing occasionally to remove from their shoes the clay that clung to them. After a while Frecks observed:

'I didn't think we'd come as far as this.'

Worrals stopped.

'You're right,' she said. 'We must have passed the machine in the murk without seeing it.

Let's go back.'

They went back a little way and then stopped again.

'This is getting us nowhere,' said Worrals in a hard voice. 'We're off our course.'

'Don't you think our best plan would be to go back to the signpost and start all over afresh?' suggested Frecks.

Worrals nodded. 'We'll try it.'

But this was easier said than done, as they were to discover. After walking for some distance they came to a field of roots which they had not previously encountered. To make matters worse, by this time it was nearly dark. Worrals shook her head.

'This is hopeless,' she said wearily. 'We're going from bad to worse. Honestly, Frecks, I could kick myself for being such a fool.'

'We ought to have had more sense than strike off blindly through the fog,' remarked Frecks miserably.

'Well, it's no use losing our heads, let's have another shot. Which way shall we go?'

'Frankly, all directions are the same to me.'

'And me,' confessed Worrals. She wetted a finger and tested the air for wind, hoping by this means to keep in a straight line. But there was not a suggestion of breeze, and presently she set off trusting, as she admitted, to luck.

For a long time they plodded on in silence. They came to a ditch, filled to the brim with turgid water, and this forced them to turn. Some time later a low hedge gave them new hope, for they thought it might lead to the clump of trees near to which the aircraft had come to rest. But they did not find the trees. Instead, they came to a narrow, poplar-lined road.

'Well, that's that,' murmured Worrals. 'I'm afraid, unless the fog lifts, we're sunk.'

'It's dark anyway, so even if the fog lifted we shouldn't be able to see very far.'

'The moon rises early,' Worrals pointed out with a cheerfulness that she was far from feeling. 'I tell you what, Frecks. Our mackintoshes cover our uniform, so if we put our caps in our pockets there would be no reason for anyone to suspect that we aren't just a couple of French girls out for a walk. If we follow this road, sooner or later we shall come to a village. It might turn out to be St. Vance. Then, by making inquiries, we ought to be able to find our way back to the leaning signpost. If we can find that we shall at least know that we're near the machine. If the village isn't St. Vance we'll ask the nearest way to it. It can't be a great distance.'

'That sounds as good as anything to me,' admitted Frecks. 'Let's go.'

'Just a minute,' said Worrals quietly. 'There's somebody coming — listen.'

They stood still, listening, while from out of the fog came the tramp of marching feet. Yet so dense was the fog that it was impossible to say for certain from which direction they were approaching.

'Lie down and don't make a sound,' ordered Worrals in a low voice.

In a moment the girls had scrambled to the side of the road, where they lay flat in the soaking grass. A few minutes later a vague shadow appeared on the road, a shadow that hardened quickly to a body of marching men. Guttural voices spoke in low tones. Heavy boots thumped a sinister tempo on the road. Frecks had a distorted view of coal scuttle helmets and sloped rifles: then, with her heart pounding against her ribs, she pressed her face in the grass. Nor did she move until the tramp of marching feet had passed on to fade away in the fog. Slowly, she raised herself on her hands and knees to see Worrals in the same position.

'I say, Worrals, this is frightful,' she groaned. 'They were real Germans.'

'They weren't shadows, you may be sure of that,' returned Worrals weakly. 'I agree with you, this is pretty awful.'

'What a sweet place home seems,' sighed

Frecks. 'Why did I leave it?'

'Because, if I remember rightly, you wanted adventure,' answered Worrals softly. 'Well, you can't complain that you aren't getting it.'

'That's just it. I'm getting too much — much too much,' faltered Frecks.

'Well, let us proceed with our plan.'

Worrals stood up, shook herself and set off at a brisk pace down the road in the direction from which the German troops had appeared. It was now quite dark, and had it not been for the silhouette of the trees against the sky they would have found it hard to keep on the road.

They walked for perhaps half a mile, and then the black outline of a village loomed up. Not a light showed. Not a soul could be seen. All was silent. Worrals went on slowly, staring at the forbidding walls on either side.

Presently they came to a corner, and a building from which emanated the murmur of voices. Worrals stood back to survey it.

'What is it?' asked Frecks.

'An *estaminet* — the local café, or tavern.'

'So what?'

As Frecks spoke the door was opened from

the inside and a man came out. He closed the door behind him, but in the brief interval that it had been open Worrals caught a glimpse of the interior. The place was, as she had stated, a tavern. Several men, including one or two German soldiers, were seated at little tables. Others lolled against a bar, from behind which a girl was serving the drinks. The man who had emerged strode away into the darkness, cursing the *Boches* under his breath.

In spite of their serious position, Worrals smiled.

'Did you hear that?' she breathed. 'That fellow, evidently a Frenchman, hates the Germans. Believe me, we shall find plenty of people in France ready and willing to help us if it is in their power. Did you see inside the bar?'

'Yes.'

'Did you notice the barmaid?'

'No.'

'It was the girl we spoke to in the lane — the girl who told us we were in France.'

'What about it?'

'She's French. I'm going in to speak to her, to ask her the way to that signpost.'

'Are you crazy?'

'Perhaps. If I'm not I soon shall be, groping about in this gloom. More chances are lost by over-caution than by taking risks. I take it as a lucky omen that we saw the girl. I'm going to follow it up. Pull yourself together and take your cues from me. My French is better than yours so you'd better leave me to do the talking. Here we go.'

Worrals opened the door and went boldly in. Frecks followed and closed the door behind them. For a moment they stood blinking in the light, shaking the moisture from their hair; then Worrals went to a vacant table and sat down. A few pairs of eyes followed them with casual curiosity; otherwise their entrance was unmarked by incident. Conversation continued unbroken, and the girl behind the bar went on serving drinks. Worrals tried to catch her eye, but for some time she was unsuccessful.

'I'm afraid she won't be able to leave the bar,' she told Frecks. 'I'll go over to her. Stay where you are.'

Worrals went to the bar and seated herself on a high stool. The girl turned to take her order.

Worrals asked for two grenadines, and when the girl brought them she said quietly, speaking of course in French:

'You remember seeing my friend and me on the road this afternoon?'

The girl nodded, smiling.

'*Oui, Mademoiselle.*'

'What village is this?'

'St. Vance.'

'So this is St. Vance. Well, we've lost our way. We are anxious to find our way back to the signpost where you saw us. Can you direct me?'

'*Certainement,*' offered the girl smilingly, and from her Worrals learned that they were less than a mile from the spot. She also ascertained which way to take when they left the *estaminet* in order to reach it.

Now, while they were speaking, Worrals saw a curious expression come into the girl's eyes, saw them switch almost furtively to where the two German soldiers were sitting, and then come back to her. Under a pretence of wiping the bar she drew nearer.

'Fasten your collar, *Mademoiselle*,' she breathed.

Worrals felt the blood drain out of her face at the significance of what this implied. Her hand went automatically to her collar, to discover that a button had come off allowing the lapels to fall open, exposing the upper part of her uniform. She tucked the two flaps together.

'*Merci, Mademoiselle*,' she said softly.

Then the barmaid had to leave her to serve more drinks, but she soon came back.

'Take care,' she whispered. 'It is dangerous here.'

Worrals knew then beyond all shadow of doubt that the girl realized, or at least suspected, what she was, and the knowledge shook her more than a little. However, it was fairly evident that the girl had no intention of betraying her, so in order to save her embarrassment she picked up the two glasses of grenadine and returned to Frecks. Naturally, as soon as she had put the glasses on the table and seated herself, she looked up to see what the girl was doing. She was no longer there! For a moment the awful thought struck her that the girl had gone to report them, but in a short time, to her infinite relief, she came back into the bar. What was more, she flashed Worrals a smile that could only be taken to mean friendliness and encouragement.

'Did you find out what we want to know?' asked Frecks impatiently.

'Yes. The barmaid knows who we are — or rather, having seen my uniform, knows we're British.'

Frecks nearly dropped her glass.

'Let's get out,' she said urgently.

'Take it easy. If you try rushing things you may create suspicion. In France people linger over their drinks. Another couple of minutes will make no difference.'

Frecks sipped her drink.

'I like this stuff — what is it?'

'Grenadine. It's a syrup — sort of takes the place of our ginger beer.'

As Worrals finished speaking the door opened and a man entered, an elderly peasant in a tattered blue blouse and greasy beret. He was unshaved; beads of moisture hung on his heavy black moustache. After greeting several of those present he sat down near the girls. The barmaid paid no further attention to them.

'All right. I think we may as well get along,' said Worrals quietly and, after finishing her drink, she had started to stand up when the door again opened, this time to admit two German officers who made straight for the bar. One of them, perched on the high stool lately vacated by Worrals, glanced round the room. His eyes met those of Frecks, and he deliberately winked. He touched his companion on the arm. and he, too, turned to survey the girls. He smiled.

'Save us!' gasped Frecks. 'They're ogling us. I'll smack their faces.'

'Don't be a fool.'

'Let's go.'

'Steady,' grated Worrals. 'Keep calm. Wait till they have their backs turned, then we'll slip out.'

Shortly afterwards the opportunity came, but before the girls could take advantage of it the door opened again and a well-dressed man came briskly into the room. He did not look beyond the two German officers, but went straight to them. In his hand he carried a small bundle — it looked like a bundle of black and white rag. This he handed to the officers, and in doing so said in a voice loud enough for the girls to hear:

'We had a job to find it owing to this infernal fog, but we got it. Here it is. I said it would come.'

Frecks' voice, low and intense, muttered:

'Worrals, do you see what I see? That black and white rag. It's a message streamer. That's the message Joudrier dropped — '

'*S-s-h.*' Worrals didn't look at Frecks. She was staring at the newcomer. His face seemed familiar to her. And as she looked she felt her limbs go cold, for she recognized him. It was the man whom they had seen with Joudrier in the Green Parrot Dance Hall.

Worrals moved quickly, turning away from the bar.

'Don't look,' she told Frecks in a swift whisper. 'Turn your back. He mustn't see our faces or we're sunk.'

Frecks, too, turned her chair so that her back was towards the bar, and Worrals, glancing at her face, knew that she, too, had recognized the man.

'I can't stand this,' breathed Frecks. 'My nerves are giving out. If he looks this way he's bound to see us.'

'He'll only see our backs, and not thinking of us, and certainly not expecting to see us here, he won't recognize us.'

'Can we get out?'

'No. We should have to pass close to him, and then he would be certain to see us. Our only chance is to sit still. He may go presently.'

In the silence that followed these words a voice, a male voice, spoke softly but distinctly — in English. It said:

'Don't look round. Listen carefully.'

Worrals stiffened with shock. She didn't move her head, but in spite of the warning she found it impossible not to switch her eyes to their nearest neighbour. It was the old French peasant in the blue blouse and greasy beret. He was staring at an advertisement that hung at an angle on the wall, while with a spoon he stirred a concoction in a small glass, sucking his teeth noisily. It seemed utterly impossible that he could have been the speaker, yet there was no one else within speaking distance.

Worrals sat still, her brain in a whirl. The whole situation was, she felt, beginning to take the unreal character of a nightmare.

The peasant yawned and, moving his hand, knocked — apparently accidentally — a draught-board and a number of pieces on the floor. He stooped clumsily to pick them up.

Again the voice spoke.

'In front of you is a curtain. Behind it is a door marked cloakroom. Go straight through to the far end. Another door will take you into the street. Turn left and wait in the church porch.'

Worrals stared at the peasant, but he didn't

even glance in their direction. Muttering thickly in low French he piled the draughts on the table and tossed back his drink, afterwards sucking his dripping moustache with gusto.

A strange feeling of calm came over Worrals.

'Are you ready, Frecks?' she said softly, knowing that she must have heard the instruction.

Came the voice again.

'Never mind about paying for your drinks.'

It gave Worrals another shock to realize that she had entered the *estaminet* and ordered refreshment without having a coin of French money in her pocket. So even if the barmaid hadn't suspected who they were, there would have been an embarrassing moment when it came to paying.

'Go now,' said the mysterious voice.

Worrals stood up, and keeping her back to the bar went to the curtain. The door was there, as the voice had said. She opened it and found herself in a corridor. It led to a woodshed, with litter of all sorts lying about. At the far side was a door. Worrals went straight to it, opened it quietly and looked up and down the street. It was deserted. She went out, and Frecks followed her.

Frecks drew a deep breath.

'Am I dreaming?' she inquired plaintively.

Worrals caught her arm.

'Come on,' she said tersely. 'We have friends here, although goodness alone knows who they are. We were told to turn left — this way.'

She set off down the street, looking up at the buildings on either side. Twenty paces and a church entrance gaped wide. She entered the black portico and came up against a heavy door. It was closed. She tried it, but it was locked. Turning to face the street she said:

'This is where we were told to wait.'

'That's okay by me,' murmured Frecks. 'I'll do anything I'm told. I'm past being able to think for myself.'

6

Friends in the Crypt

For ten minutes the girls cowered in their chilly retreat, listening intently for footsteps to approach from the direction of the *estaminet*. Occasionally they spoke, in whispers. Frecks would have discussed the situation, but Worrals wanted to think. There was plenty to occupy her mind. She no longer had any doubt about Joudrier being a spy; the dropping of the message in enemy-occupied territory proved that conclusively. He was, as Major Gray had surmised, the connecting link between enemy agents operating in England, and agents on the Continent. His companion of the Green Parrot Dance Hall was clearly one of the gang, although how he had got across the Channel so quickly was a mystery. Worrals concluded that he must have flown across — perhaps landed by parachute.

Then there was the queer French peasant who

had spoken to them. He could only be a British agent. How had he known they were British? Pondering the question, Worrals remembered the barmaid going through to the back room immediately after speaking to her. It rather looked as if the girl, too, was acting for the British, and had passed word on to the peasant, who had, Worrals remembered, appeared shortly afterwards. Taking it all round, it seemed likely that the district of St. Vance was the French end of the line of enemy agents, as the Green Parrot was the opposite end in Britain. But if enemy agents were at work, British agents were at work, too. And into this sinister network of espionage the girls had blundered — all because of so small a thing as a geranium leaf.

Worrals, peering anxiously into the gloom, could have smiled at the incongruity of it all. The trouble was, she perceived, they did not fit into the scheme. They were just as likely to get in the way of the British agents as the enemy operatives. So engrossed was she in watching the pavement that she forgot all about the church porch behind her, and she started nervously when a key grated in a heavy lock. She stepped quickly

against the wall, pulling Frecks with her, as a
hinge squeaked, announcing that the door was
being opened. There was something ominous in
the sound.

'Are you there?' said a voice quietly, in
English.

'Yes,' answered Worrals.

'Come in.'

The girls stepped into the coal-black interior,
and then stood still, in utter darkness, while the
door was relocked. Then a tiny torch flung an
eerie glow on the stone-flagged floor. It moved
slowly down the aisle.

'Follow me,' said the voice in the darkness.

The interior of a church, at night, is always
impressive. In the circumstances it was almost
unnerving. The silence, the faint but cloying
aroma of incense, the unseen distances, all
combined to create an atmosphere of medieval
mystery and intrigue. Worrals was very conscious
of it as she followed the pale glow down the aisle.

The light came to rest on what at first appeared
to be a tomb, but looking closely Worrals saw that
it was the entrance to a crypt. Their guide, whom
they were still unable to see, rapped on it sharply

— a double knock, thrice repeated. A moment later the stone swung slowly open to disclose an elderly man with a grave, cultured face. His sombre habit revealed his calling. He was a priest — presumably the *curé* of the church. He made a sign for them to enter, holding a hand towards a flight of stone steps that led downwards. Not without some slight qualms Worrals descended, Frecks following close behind. The steps were short, and ended in a fairly extensive chamber, lighted by tall candles.

To say that Worrals was surprised at the scene that now met her eyes would be an understatement. She was astounded. She had followed the guide unquestioningly — in the circumstances she could hardly do otherwise; but she had imagined that he was leading the way to a place where they could talk without interruption. What was her amazement, then, to find herself the cynosure of about a dozen pairs of questioning eyes. Not fewer than twelve men — she didn't trouble to count them — were seated about the room on forms, stools, and church kneelers.

After a single penetrating stare, Worrals turned eyes, round with wonder, on the *curé*, and the man who had guided them to the crypt. She was not surprised to see that he was the untidy peasant. He must have observed the interrogation in her eyes, for he made haste to reassure her.

'Don't worry,' he said casually, in faultless Oxford English. 'You are among friends.'

The *curé* smiled faintly.

'You have nothing to fear,' he murmured, in the same language.

'But who are all these men?' asked Worrals in a low voice.

'Look again, and your eyes should answer that question,' said the peasant.

Worrals looked, and understanding dawned in her expression. The men were all in uniforms — or what had once been uniforms. Most of them were British Tommies, but there was a sprinkling of Air Force blue. A few had evidently been wounded, for they wore bandages.

'They are some of the chaps who were cut off from Dunkirk,' said the peasant softly. 'There are still scores in hiding all over northern France, having found French people willing to risk their lives and liberty by concealing them. We have been getting them home as fast as we can. Those you see here were collected by the good padre, Father Giraldus.'

'Has any arrangement been made to get them home?'

'Not yet.'

'If I can get home I'll see that something is done about it,' declared Worrals.

'And now,' went on the peasant curiously, 'perhaps you will be good enough to tell me who you are, how you came to be here, and what you are doing? You hardly look like refugees.'

'We're not,' answered Worrals frankly. 'But before I answer your question I would prefer to know who you are.'

'For the moment you will have to take me on trust. You can call me Captain Charles.'

'Very well,' murmured Worrals. 'We're not refugees in the sense that these boys are, although it rather looks as if we soon shall be. I was delivering an aircraft in England but was blown off my course by a gale of wind. I couldn't see the ground when the engine packed up and I had to make a forced landing. Then I found that I was in France. As soon as we knew that we tried to get back to our machine in the hope of repairing it before dawn, but we got lost in the fog and stumbled on this place. The girl behind the counter told me how to find my way back to the machine, which is near a leaning signpost. We were just going back to it when that man came in and spoke to the German officers. Did you notice that he carried a message bag? I can't go into details, but I happen to know that the bag was dropped by a pilot flying a British aircraft.'

The man who called himself Captain Charles looked up sharply.

'You mean — the man was a spy. . . that there is a message in that bag?'

'Undoubtedly.'

'Then I must try to recover it. But what about the man — the spy?'

'AII I can tell you is, he was in England last night. We saw him.'

'Ah! Thank you. This is important information. I must try to recover that bag. You had better wait here — unless you would prefer to stick to your original plan of repairing the aircraft. But you realize, of course, that if you fail, you will be captured as soon as it gets light. The country is stiff with German troops. If they take you, it will be almost impossible for us to help you.'

'All the same, I'd rather take the chance of getting away than being stuck here,' declared Worrals without hesitation. 'By Jove! I wonder . . . ? I might kill two birds with one stone.'

She turned quickly to the airmen who were among the refugees.

'Do any of you boys happen to be fitters?' she inquired.

A cheerful ginger-headed youth stood up.

'I'm a fitter — aero, miss,' he said, with a strong Cockney accent.

'Do you know the Merlin engine?'

'I ought to — I've done two years on them.'

Hope thrilled in Worrals' voice.

'Do you feel like snatching at a chance of getting home?'

The lad grinned.

'Give me the chance!'

'Right! This is the position,' went on Worrals quickly, and told of the aircraft with the faulty engine. 'If you can put it right before dawn we ought to be able to get away. With any luck we'll have breakfast in England,' she concluded.

There was a murmur among the men.

'I can only take one,' said Worrals regretfully. 'But if we get away, I promise that a plane will come and fetch you all — if I have to fly it myself. How's that?'

There was a buzz of excitement, followed by an argument, for some of the men were in favour of forming a sort of protective cordon round the machine while the fitter worked on it. But to this Worrals would not agree.

'You will all stay here with the padre', she ordered.

Captain Charles touched her on the arm.

'I'm going now. I may see you again, or I may not. Anyway, good luck. The padre has offered to guide you to the leaning signpost — he knows where it is, of course.'

'That's splendid!' cried Worrals enthusiastically. She turned to Frecks, who had been a witness of the arrangement. 'Our luck seems to be in.'

Said the padre: 'The sooner we start the better.'

'We are ready,' announced Worrals.

'Not a sound after we leave the crypt',

cautioned the padre. 'Remember, this is France, and in France today any wall or hedge may have ears and eyes.'

The cockney fitter tightened his belt and buttoned his tunic. His face split in a broad grin.

'Blimey! This is a bit of orl right,' he chuckled.

'It should be, if you can fix the engine,' agreed Worrals.

'Leave it to me, miss.'

'By the way, what's your name?'

'The boys call me Tim.'

'Okay, Tim.' Worrals turned to the padre. 'Lead on, Father,' she said in French.

The padre smiled. 'You speak French?'

'Yes.'

'It may be useful.'

'It has been already.'

'This way.'

Silently the padre led the way back into the church, and closed the door of the crypt behind him. As Worrals glanced for the last time round the circle of serious faces that she was leaving behind she made a mental vow that if it was within her power she would secure their release.

The padre, carrying a torch, passed on to the

main entrance. With infinite caution he opened the door a few inches and listened.

'Come,' he whispered.

The little party went out, and with no more noise than shadows moved off into the mist. They walked in single file, keeping close, for the fog still clung to the ground and the darkness was intense. Not a light showed anywhere. The moon and stars were, of course, hidden behind the blanket of clammy moisture. Turning into a lane they went on more quickly. The only sound was the soft rasping of shoes on gravel. So dark was it that it gave Worrals a shock to realize how futile it would have been for them to attempt to find the signpost without a guide.

After about twenty minutes of steady walking the padre halted.

'Here is the signpost,' he whispered. 'You will have to help me now. Where is the machine?'

'About a hundred yards from here there is a wood.'

'Yes, I know it.'

'The aircraft is close under it, on the left hand side as we face it from here. The field in which it stands has been ploughed, I think, although the rain has washed it fairly flat.'

'That should enable me to find it,' murmured the padre, and went on.

Soon the girls felt soft earth under their feet. For five minutes they went on, slowly, and then the padre halted again.

'Listen,' he breathed. In a silence so intense that it seemed to worry the eardrums, the little party stood still, listening. Seconds passed. Then, from a short distance in front, came a sound. It was the low mutter of voices.

'I'm afraid we are too late,' whispered the padre sadly. 'There must be at least two people by the machine otherwise there would be no talking.'

Worrals' heart sank.

'They may be French people.'

'It is possible,' admitted the padre.

'We'd better find out before we do anything else,' breathed Worrals. 'If they are French they may help us — or at least they won't raise an alarm.'

'If they are French they will do as I tell them, I think,' said the padre.

'Then wait here,' returned Worrals, and crept

away into the darkness.

Frecks shivered. The old nightmare feeling came back. She found it hard to believe that the situation was real; it was too fantastic, too eerie. Yet, strangely enough, she was not in the least afraid. Her paramount sensation was one of suspense. She felt that something must happen at any moment. Standing there in the gloom, with the two shadowy figures beside her, two men who an hour before she did not know existed, she lost count of time. It seemed an age before Worrals returned.

'I don't understand it,' she said. 'The machine is there, and one man, standing by the wing.'

'Only one?' said the padre in a puzzled voice.

'Yes, he stands there alone, silent, as though on guard.'

'German or French?'

'I'm not sure — German I think. There can only be one; if there were more, surely they would be talking.'

'They did talk just now.'

'I've got it,' put in Tim. 'They must have stumbled on the machine by accident — two of them. One's gone to report it, and the other has stayed to keep watch. That's how I should work it out if me and a pal found a Jerry plane.'

'Yes, I think that's the answer,' agreed Worrals.

'The man who has gone for help may be some time finding his way to his camp, or to the village,' put in the padre. 'Moreover, like you, he may find it difficult to locate the machine again.'

'But what about the man who is there?' asked Worrals.

'Leave him to me,' muttered Tim grimly.

'What are you going to do?' asked Worrals quickly.

'After what the Jerries did to me and my pals I've been pining for the day when I could get a crack at one.'

As Tim spoke he drew something from his pocket and balanced it in his hand.

'You mustn't make a noise,' said Worrals firmly.

'There won't be no noise, miss,' promised Tim, and then faded into the murky background.

'This is getting positively shocking,' faltered Frecks.

'You'll think so if the Huns catch us,' replied

Worrals sharply. 'We can't afford to be squeamish. Anyway, people who barge into a war must expect to see something of the seamy side. Frankly, I'm only concerned with getting home, and if a few Huns get hurt on the way I shan't saturate my pillow with tears on their account.'

Tim's voice came out of the darkness.

'Oky-doke,' he called cheerfully.

Frecks let out a gasp, the sound was so unexpected; but she stumbled on after the others as they moved forward. The dark outline of the aircraft loomed up. Tim was standing by the nose. Of the guard there was no sign.

'Was it a Jerry?' asked Frecks.

'Too true it was,' returned Tim.

'Where is he?'

Tim chuckled. 'Having forty winks.'

'Will he — ever wake up?'

'I reckon so,' murmured Tim regretfully. 'If he's fool enough to wake up before his time I shall have to put him to sleep again.'

'Where did you put him?'

'In the bushes. Now let's get on with the job. I may need some 'elp. You'd better borrow the parson's torch, miss — I shall work faster with a light. It'll be safe enough. Visibility ain't more than ten yards in this pea soup.'

Worrals borrowed the padre's torch, and suggested that he now returned to the church. But he would not go. He announced his intention of staying to see the end of the affair. So Worrals asked him to keep guard on one side of the machine, while Frecks watched on the other side. Then she joined Tim at the engine.

He asked her to describe precisely the manner in which the engine had failed, and she did so. 'There was no warning,' she said. 'That's why I think it's ignition trouble.'

'Sounds like it,' agreed Tim, and went to work.

For the best part of an hour there was practically no sound as he explored the ignition leads. Then, with infinite satisfaction, he announced that he had found the trouble.

'Can you put it right?' asked Worrals anxiously.

'I think so, but without proper tackle it will 'ave to be a temporary job, and it may take some time.'

'How long?'

'Couple of hours, I should say.'

'The torch won't last all that time. The battery is giving out.'

'Then we'll 'ave to do our best,' declared Tim optimistically.

Worrals had no idea of the time, but from the padre she learned that they still had about three hours until dawn would set a limit on their activities. She turned to Tim and passed on the information.

'That ought to be long enough,' he said brightly.

Worrals thought of the German who they assumed had gone to fetch assistance, but she said nothing. Fascinated, she watched Tim's deft fingers working on the complicated ignition system of the engine. For what seemed an eternity of time he worked ceaselessly, and Frecks, standing by the wing tip, expected dawn to break at any moment. There were moments when she rather hoped it would, for she was cold, wet and tired beyond imagination. From time to time she shook the clinging moisture from her hair, or wiped it from her eyes. She started violently when, at no great distance, the long silence was at last broken by a hail.

Running round to the fuselage she met Worrals.

'What was that?' she gasped.

The padre hurried up.

'I'm afraid it's the enemy, looking for the machine — no doubt the man who went to fetch help.'

Worrals clenched her fists in her agitation.

'That's bad luck,' she muttered. 'We had nearly finished. Another five minutes would have seen the job done.'

'Then there's still a chance,' exclaimed the padre. 'When the man who was left here doesn't answer the hail the others will suspect that all is not well, so we must answer for him. They are having difficulty in finding the machine on account of the fog. I shall endeavour to lead them away from it. Good-bye and good luck.'

Father Giraldus gathered his skirts about him and sped away into the fog, now slowly turning grey with the approach of dawn. Presently the girls heard him call out.

His voice was answered by a call of surprise.

Again came the padre's voice, farther away.

Again came the answering voices, also at a distance.

There was another hail from the padre — faint, now. And so it went on, the cries becoming fainter and fainter.

'By Jove! He's drawing them away,' declared Worrals. 'He's a brave man.'

She ran to the nose of the machine.

'How does it go, Tim?'

'Okay — I hope. You can start her up now.'

Tim jumped to the ground, wiping his hands on his slacks.

'Stand by,' ordered Worrals. 'Goodness knows what's in front of us, but there's no wind, so I can take off the way I came in — there must be a fair run. We shall have to risk it, anyway.'

Worrals threw a quick glance at the now lightening sky and climbed into the cockpit.

'Be ready to get aboard in a hurry,' she called. Her voice ended in a shout for, as it grew swiftly lighter, she turned her eyes upwards and saw the reason. The fog was lifting.

Into the next two or three minutes was packed the excitement of a lifetime. Would the engine start? Upon that single fact everything now depended. Automatically Worrals went through the usual routine for starting up. Now. . .?

With a roar the engine sprang to life. She steadied it with the throttle and then looked about her, desperately anxious to see the lie of the land. She also intended calling to the others to get aboard, for as yet no arrangement had been made, and it would be necessary for Tim to squeeze into the gunner's seat with Frecks. But at the sight that met her gaze her throat seemed to become paralysed.

The fog had lifted, and was still rising, leaving the landscape comparatively clear. A bare hundred yards away, a line of men, strung out like runners at the end of a race, were running towards the aircraft. They shouted as they ran.

7

Worrals Keeps A Promise

After the first stunning shock of this discovery had passed, Worrals acted swiftly. She yelled to the others to get aboard, and dropping into her seat pushed the throttle open. Jamming on one brake she swung the machine round in its own length to face the open field. This was the direction from which the Germans were coming, but there was no alternative because the group of trees made a take-off in any other direction impossible.

Tim reached the gunner's seat first, but waited for Frecks to get aboard. He was laughing hilariously, although what he found to laugh at in such a situation was beyond Worrals' understanding.

'Home, James,' he shouted, and followed Frecks into the machine.

By this time the nearest German, a heavily

built officer, was a bare fifty yards away. With a revolver in his hand he was shooting as he ran. The first shots must have gone wide, for Worrals neither heard nor felt anything of them; but then one struck the windscreen with a crash that made her catch her breath. She pushed the throttle wide open. The engine roared. The tail lifted and the aircraft sped across the wet earth like a winged torpedo, straight towards the Germans. There could be no question of turning to avoid

them, for to attempt to turn an aircraft on the ground when travelling at high speed is to invite disaster.

At the last moment the Germans flung themselves flat. What happened to them after that Worrals did not know: she was too concerned with what she was doing. The machine swayed as it bumped off a low ridge of rising ground; for a moment it sagged bodily as though on the point of stalling, then became steadily airborne and soared into the air. For a mile Worrals kept on a straight course, reminded of her full load by a slight sluggishness of the controls; then she turned slowly towards the north. Below her lay the village with its radiating lanes; on one of them stood a black-robed figure, face upturned, and Worrals knew that the padre was safe.

Still climbing, she scrutinized the sky carefully in every direction for hostile aircraft, but as far as she could see she was alone in the sky. Not that she could see very far, for the billowing clouds of mist still drifted overhead. Levelling out just under it she flew on, keeping an anxious look-out for the channel, which she felt could not be far away. On all sides lay the flat, hedgeless landscape that is peculiar to northern France and, considering it, she saw that her blind forced landing had not been so remarkable after all. It would have been possible to land almost anywhere. However, as a spectacle she held a poor view of it, and she smiled faintly with satisfaction when it ended abruptly at a sandy beach washed by a line of weary waves. Beyond lay the sea, a leaden carpet unbroken by any sort of craft.

But the water was not the only thing that appeared. Suddenly the sky was torn with flames that left behind them clouds of oily black smoke. Worrals was not surprised. Even if the presence of the British aircraft had not been reported by the Germans at St. Vance, which was likely, she would have had to run the gauntlet of flak when crossing the coast so low. In a way, she was glad the flak was there, for it suggested that there were no hostile aircraft in the immediate neighbourhood. But even as she roared over the beach and headed out to sea the fog dispersed suddenly, as it sometimes will. The ceiling overhead turned faintly blue, and a watery sun peered mistily at the scene.

What made Worrals look behind she did not

know; it may have been instinct, for to nothing else can be attributed that awareness of danger that comes in moments of peril. Be that as it may, glancing back over her tail she started when she saw, not far behind and slightly above, the outlines of three aircraft which she recognized instantly as Messerschmitts. That they had seen her, and were in pursuit; was obvious. As yet they were out of range, and knowing the futility of attempting to out-climb them she thrust the control column forward in the hope of widening the gap. The trouble was that, not knowing exactly where she had crossed the coast, she did not know how far she still had to fly before sanctuary, in the shape of the English shore, could be expected.

Looking back again over her shoulder she saw the Messerschmitts diving to the attack. Behind them there was now another machine, and at first she assumed that the Messerschmitt pilots had been joined by a comrade. Then she saw that she had been mistaken. The fourth machine was not a Messerschmitt; it was a Reliant like her own.

What happened after that she was not quite clear.

Snatching a glance ahead she saw the British coast materialize out of the tenuous mist that had hidden it; and by the time she had turned her head to look again at the pursuing aircraft the position had entirely altered. Two were heading back towards France. Another, the Reliant, was nearly alongside. Its identification letter identified it as Bill's machine. She did not see what became of the other Messerschmitt.

There was no more trouble and shortly afterwards, feeling suddenly very tired, she landed safely on the home aerodrome. Bill followed her in, and her first words were, as he jumped down and joined them:

'Thanks, Bill. It was a bit of luck you happened to be about.'

Bill frowned.

'What do you mean — luck?' he inquired curtly. 'Do you suppose I was fooling about over the French coast by accident? I was looking for you.'

'Looking for me?' cried Worrals incredulously.

'Of course.'

'But how on earth did you know I was there?'

'As a matter of fact, I didn't know for certain.

When Joudrier took off yesterday afternoon I followed him to see where he went. When I got up through the clouds I saw him heading south with you in pursuit. I roared along after you, trying to head you off because I guessed from the way you were flying that you had no idea you were being blown over France. Before I could do anything about it, though, you went down through the murk with a Messerschmitt on your tail. I hung about for a bit, but the fog prevented me from doing anything. When you didn't come back I knew you were down in France.'

'Quite right, I was. What happened to Joudrier?'

'He came back — in fact, we flew home together.'

'Did you see him drop that message?'

Bill's frown deepened. He shook his head.

'No, I didn't see anything. I was too concerned with what was happening to you.'

'Where's Joudrier now?'

'I suppose he's on the station somewhere. But tell me, what happened to you?'

At this point the conversation was interrupted by a messenger from the squadron office who informed Worrals and Frecks that their presence was required immediately by the C.O.

Bill jerked his thumb towards Tim, who had emerged from the machine.

'Who's this fellow?'

'Oh, that's Tim,' answered Worrals.

'Where did you pick him up?'

'In France.'

'In *France*?'

'That's what I said.'

Bill shrugged his shoulders helplessly.

'I'm going crazy,' he muttered.

'You'd have gone crazy had you been with us last night,' declared Worrals. 'I haven't time to tell you about it now — the C.O.'s waiting for us. I suppose he knows we didn't come back Iast night?'

'Of course he knows! You're on the "missing" list.'

'Did you tell him anything? I mean, about us, and Joudrier?'

'No. I didn't know what to say and that's a fact. But I should have told him today if you hadn't turned up.'

'Well, we'd better get along.'

Worrals beckoned to Frecks and walked off in the direction of the squadron office.

'You'd better come too,' she told Tim. 'I'm afraid we shall have to confess the truth, and you'll be able to support our story.'

'I might as well come and complete the party,' grumbled Bill. 'There's going to be a lovely row — and you can't blame the C.O. for that. You won't mind my remarking that I think you two kids are as mad as hatters.'

'I'm afraid you're right, Bill,' agreed Worrals sadly, as they all entered the C.O.'s office together.

Squadron-Leader McNavish was waiting. His eyes were frostier than usual; his expression was hostile, and his crouching attitude belligerent. He considered Worrals with frank disfavour.

'So you've decided to come back — very condescending of you,' he said with biting sarcasm.

Worrals knew the C.O. too well to answer.

'Well, what have you got to say?' snapped the C.O.

Worrals moistened her lips.

'Well, sir — '

'Well, eh? It isn't well.'

The C.O. fairly spat the words.

'Very good, sir.'

'Very good — ha! I'm glad you think so.'

Worrals flushed. She perceived that explanations were going to be difficult. Still, knowing the C.O. better perhaps than he knew himself she was patient.

'Do you want to hear my story, sir?' she asked mildly.

'No,' snapped the C.O. 'But because I happen to command this unit I suppose I shall have to. Where have you been?'

'To France, sir.'

The C.O. started as though he had been stung by a wasp. 'To *where*?'

'France, sir.'

'Yes, you said that before.' The C.O.'s eyes wandered round the party. They came to rest on Tim — and opened wide. 'Jones! Where the deuce have you sprung from? I thought you'd been killed.'

'Oh no, sir, not me,' returned Tim. 'The Jerries couldn't kill me.'

'They were having a thundering good try the last time I saw you,' declared the C.O. 'What happened to you?'

'I got cut off, sir. This young lady just brought me home in her plane.'

The C.O. shook his head.

'What a war,' he breathed. Yet the sight of Tim appeared to have taken the edge off his temper, for he looked at Bill, and said by way of explanation: 'Jones, here, was in my squadron in France, when the crack-up came.'

He turned again to Worrals.

'What happened to you?' It seemed that at last curiosity had overcome all other emotions.

Worrals hesitated.

'It's rather difficult to explain, sir. You see, I'm more or less tied by a promise — '

'It's all right, Miss Worralson. You'd better tell the whole story,' put in a quiet voice.

Worrals spun round. Sitting in a chair, smoking a cigarette, was Major Gray.

'You here?' she gasped.

'Yes. Things have been happening since you went away, and I found it essential to take Squadron-Leader McNavish into my confidence.'

'Then he knows what I told you?'

'Yes, I know all about your trip to London,'

rasped the C.O. 'Why can't you stick to your job instead of crashing in on other people's business? All right — we're all waiting. What happened?'

Worrals told her story, starting from the time she took off the previous evening and ending with her flight home across the Channel. Once she nearly laughed at the expression on the C.O.'s face. When she had finished the Squadron-Leader looked at Major Gray.

'Did you ever hear anything like that?' he muttered. 'How does this fit in with what you know?'

'Perfectly,' Major Gray came forward. 'I must tell you,' he said, speaking directly to Worrals, 'that largely as a result of the information you gave us about Joudrier, which supplied certain missing evidence, we made a raid last night. We raided the Green Parrot Dance Hall, which was a rendezvous of spies, and the ice cream factory, which was really their headquarters. We made a nice bag, but two men slipped through the net. One was the man you saw at the Green Parrot with Joudrier, and the other was Joudrier himself. We know now that he is not a Belgian, but a German.'

Worrals looked disappointed.

'How did he get away?'

'I'm not sure yet that he has got away. I came down here with a warrant for his arrest, only to find that he had just departed on seven days' leave.'

'But he must know by now that his game is up?'

'Probably. But we shall catch him. He can't get out of the country.'

'Why can't he? His friend — the Green Parrot man — is in France. I saw him there last night.'

'That may be so, but he's the last man who will travel by that route. He escaped by air. We have details of the organization, and that bolt-hole is now definitely stopped. I'm sure you will understand if I say that I can't go into details about that. There is just a chance that Joudrier, not knowing that he is suspected, may come back here.'

'But if he goes to the Green Parrot, as he probably will, he'll learn about the raid.'

'If he goes to the Green Parrot he will be arrested. My men are still there.'

Worrals nodded.

'I see. There's one question I'd like to ask. To what point across the Channel were these air spies operating?'

'That's something I can't tell you.'

'You can't, or you won't?'

'I can't.'

'Then shall I tell you?'

Major Gray looked surprised.

'You know?'

'No, but I imagine it's St. Vance, the village where I was last night. Why else should Joudrier's friend be there? That's where Joudrier dropped the message bag, too, don't forget.'

'By Jove! You're right,' agreed Major Gray thoughtfully.

'The only thing against that is, why didn't your agent there discover the plot and report it?'

'Agent?'

'The dirty little Frenchman I told you about — the man who calls himself Captain Charles.'

Major Gray looked puzzled.

'I don't know anything about him,' he confessed. 'He may be one of our fellows or he may not. When the French collapsed a lot of British people found themselves stranded, so he

may be a civilian acting on his own account, working with the padre, taking care of these stranded
soldiers and airmen.'

'Which reminds me, I have promised to get
those boys home.'

The C.O. raised his eyebrows.

'Oh, you have?'

'Yes, sir,'

'Upon my life, young lady, you make some
rash promises.'

'I don't see that it's rash, sir,' protested
Worrals. 'All we need is a big aircraft — a
Wellington, for instance. I could go over — '

'Rubbish. It's no job for a girl.'

'We haven't done badly so far, sir,' reminded
Worrals.

'You always have an answer ready,' sighed
the C.O.

'If I may put in a word, I think she's right, sir,'
declared Bill, speaking for the first time.

'Why?'

'Because the job would have to be done at
night, and a stranger would have a dickens of a
job to find his way. I know the village. I could fly
a machine over.'

'But somebody would have to go over first and warn the boys to be ready.'

'That could be my job, sir,' put in Worrals quickly. 'This is my plan. Flying Officer Ashton can fly me over after dark. I'll land by parachute, get hold of Captain Charles, and bring the boys along. Or I could find the padre. With his help I could collect the boys and take them to the landing field at a pre-arranged time — say at midnight. Flying Officer Ashton is in the air with the big machine. I send a signal by torchlight that we are ready. He lands, and we all come home together. It sounds perfectly simple.'

'It may sound that way to you,' muttered the C.O.

'Paxton and Hilton are there, sir,' put in Tim. 'You remember them? They were in the old squadron.'

The C.O. stroked his chin.

'The dickens they are? Two good men. Hm.'

Worrals winked at Bill, realizing that the C.O. was wavering.

'Naturally, I should have to get Air Ministry permission before undertaking such an operation,' the C.O. pointed out.

'Of course, sir,' agreed Bill blandly, 'but since we are all volunteers it seems unlikely that any objection will be raised. The rescue of a dozen chaps from the clutches of the Hun would make a first class story for the newspapers.'

The C.O. waved his hand.

'All right. I'll see what I can do.' He turned to Major Gray. 'Is there anything else I can do for you?'

'No — unless, of course, Joudrier comes back. If he does, put him under guard and let me know. Otherwise, as far as I'm concerned, the affair is finished.'

The Major turned to Worrals and held out his hand. 'Thanks for your help,' he said. 'If people used their heads as you do, spying in this country would be more difficult than it is.' He smiled. 'If you can grab Joudrier's Green Parrot friend and bring him back with you, I could do with a few words with him,' he said jokingly.

Worrals laughed. 'I'll see what I can do about it,' she promised, and with that Major Gray departed.

'All right, that's all,' said the C.O. 'Jones, you'd better go and get yourself something to eat and get the quartermaster to fix you up with some new kit. You girls had better go and get some sleep — you look as though you can do with it. Ashton, you stay here. I want to talk to you.'

Worrals and Frecks turned towards the door. As soon as they were outside Frecks turned to Worrals. 'I notice you didn't include me in your plan for the rescue,' she said coldly. 'You don't suppose I'm going to be left out, do you?'

'But there's no reason for two to go. One can do the job.'

'Isn't there?' inquired Frecks acidly. 'Where would you be without me to do the dirty work?'

Worrals laughed.

'Come by all means if the C.O.'ll let you,' she agreed. 'It isn't for me to decide. Naturally I'd rather have you with me — you help to keep the party bright.'

Worrals spoke casually, but the truth was, she had no delusions about the danger of the enterprise upon which she proposed to embark, and she was too fond of Frecks willingly to let her take unnecessary risks.

The subject was not pursued, for they both were too tired to argue. They walked on to their quarters, had a bath, and were just getting into bed when an orderly brought Worrals a message.

'What's that?' asked Frecks suspiciously.

'It's from Bill,' answered Worrals. 'The show is fixed for tonight. We are using the Wellington. He's going to fly me over, leaving the ground at nine o'clock.'

'You mean he's going to fly *us* over,' grunted Frecks, as she fell into bed.

8

Parachute Jump

At a quarter to nine, refreshed by a sound sleep, the girls met Bill outside the officers' mess. He had already been busy, for a big Havelock troop carrier, sinister in its sable camouflage, stood on the tarmac. Bill, who was in flying kit, told them that he had decided that a Havelock would suit their purpose better than a Wellington.

With him was another officer whom the girls did not know, but who was introduced to them as a member of the Air Intelligence staff. Although he was not to take part in the expedition he had more than a passing interest in it, for he represented the Air Ministry, which — so the girls were informed — regarded the rescue attempt as an experiment that might, if successful, be developed.

The girls were dressed as they had been on the occasion of their last visit to France — that is, in uniforms well concealed by raincoats. Worrals had considered wearing civilian clothes, in order that they might pass as French girls if they were seen, but this the C.O. had promptly vetoed, pointing out that if they were caught in 'civvies' they would certainly suffer the penalty of spies, whereas in uniform they would be able to assert that they were engaged in a purely military operation, and so be able to claim the privileges of prisoners of war.

The final plan was much as Worrals had originally outlined it, except that permission had been obtained for Frecks to go with her. They were to be taken over St. Vance in the Havelock, which Bill would fly. They would descend by parachute after which he would return home. At twelve midnight he would fly again to St. Vance, and watch for the letter V to be signalled by a red flash lamp. This would be the signal that the party was at the field waiting to be picked up. Bill would then land, collect his passengers and take off immediately. If all went well there would be no need for him to be on the ground for more than five minutes.

There had been some slight argument when

the C.O. had learned that Worrals wanted to take Frecks with her — or perhaps it would be more correct to say that Frecks wanted to go. The C.O. had asserted, with a truth that Worrals had found hard to deny, that there was no need to risk two lives when one could do all that was required, but Worrals, feeling compelled to support Frecks' claim, had pointed out that apart from an unexpected emergency, the moral support of having a trusty comrade would go far to ensure success. So the C.O., declaring that the organization of the 'show' was Worrals' affair, had given in.

Worrals was confident of success. She could not see how the scheme could fail unless unlooked-for factors arose to throw the whole plan out of gear. An important item was the weather. Fog or heavy rain would make Bill's already hazardous night landing doubly dangerous. In the event of such a contingency he was to return home and repeat the programme at the same hour on the following night. In that case, of course, the girls would have to seek sanctuary in the church, or find some other hiding-place. At the moment the weather was all that could be desired. There was a fair amount of cloud about, which could be used as cover for the aircraft in emergency; yet it was broken, and through gaps the stars, and a slim crescent moon, gave just enough light for the undertaking.

Bill looked at his watch.

'Zero hour,' he said. 'If you kids are ready we'll be off.'

'We're ready — but not so much of the kids,' returned Worrals.

The C.O. appeared — as did most of the officers on the station — and wished them good luck. They had never seen him so concerned. As Frecks remarked, as they followed Bill to the aircraft, he seemed almost human.

The girls, of course, had worn parachutes before, for this was part of ordinary routine; but neither of them had ever made a deliberate jump. And it was not until the harness was being adjusted that they — or Frecks at any rate — realized the nature of the ordeal in front of them. It was not a question of the 'brollies' being a possible safety device. They were definitely, in cold blood, to be used. However, there was no going back now, and neither of the girls made any comment as, with the heavy packs harnessed to their slim bodies, they took their places in the Havelock. The door was closed. Bill went through to the cockpit. From the roomy cabin the girls could see his face, pale in the glow of the luminous instruments.

He looked worried, and Worrals went through to him.

'Feeling all right, Bill?' she inquired.

'No, I'm not,' snapped Bill.

Worrals started.

'What's the matter?' she asked with genuine concern.

'I don't like the idea of you doing this job.' Bill's manner was curt.

'It's a bit late in the day to start talking like that. What's come over you?'

Bill turned in his seat and looked up into Worrals' face.

'Don't you know?'

'No — how should I?'

Bill seemed to have difficulty in speaking.

'Well, it's you,' he blurted.

'Me?'

'Yes, you. You know, kid, you mean an awful lot to me. If anything happened to you on this show I should never forgive myself.'

Bill caught Worrals' hand, and held it. For a moment Worrals stared in genuine surprise. Then, recovering herself, 'Bill.' she said, 'you're not by any chance making love to me, are you?'

'Call it that if you like.'

'But, Bill! Couldn't you think of a better time and place to start this sort of conversation than in the cockpit of an aircraft with the entire squadron standing round?'

'It wasn't until I saw you with that brolly on, and realized that you might not come back — '

'Hey, wait a minute, Bill,' broke in Worrals. 'Do you want me to burst into tears? Be yourself. You'll laugh at this nonsense in the morning.'

'I hope you're right,' returned Bill moodily.

Frecks' face appeared in the bulkhead doorway.

'What's going on?' she demanded. Then, after a glance at Bill's face, and Worrals' in turn: 'Well, for the love of Mike! Have you two gone crazy? What is this, anyway — a musical comedy? I thought they only did this sort of thing on the flicks. I'm in this party, don't forget. If there's going to be any sob-stuff I'll bale out now, while

I've only three feet to jump.'

Worrals laughed, and it broke the tension.

'Go ahead, Bill,' she said, and returned to the cabin. A minute later the aircraft vibrated as the twin engine came to life with a roar. Then it began to creep forward into the darkness.

'Well, here we go,' murmured Frecks. Worrals felt in her pocket and produced a packet of chocolate.

'Have some,' she invited. 'It's a bit of pre-war nut-milk.'

'Where did you get it?' inquired Frecks, helping herself generously.

'Oh, I had a bar or two tucked away in reserve for some big occasion, and this seems to be it.'

'Yes, I guess we might as well eat it while the going's good,' agreed Frecks.

Then the engines burst into full song and the machine roared up into the starry sky.

'We're on our way,' announced Frecks, munching steadily. 'I hope we don't run into a chunk of flak.'

'Bill will take care of that,' returned Worrals confidently. 'He's going up to 20,000 before he crosses the coast. Empty, this machine should make easy work of it. It's going to be chilly presently, that's why I had a couple of rugs put in.'

The machine droned on. The girls fell silent. Worrals was thinking about Bill's last words, which really only confirmed what she had long suspected. After a time she stood up and gazed down at the black countryside below. The people down there, she thought, were in another world. She could imagine anxious faces upturned, wondering if the aircraft was British, or an enemy. Occasionally searchlight beams stabbed the darkness, cutting the sky into wedge-shaped patterns. She glanced at the altimeter with which the cabin was provided, and then reached for the rugs.

'It's getting parky,' she announced. A little later she went through to the cockpit and sank into the spare seat next to Bill. 'Feeling better?' she asked.

'I shall feel better when I've got you safe back home,' muttered Bill.

'Upon my life you're positively depressing,' protested Worrals.

Bill threw her a glance, and a smile.

'Sorry, kid — don't take any notice of me. I

had to tell you though.'

'Don't apologize, Bill — I like it,' answered Worrals, and bolted back to the cabin.

Frecks considered her reflectively.

'What are you getting all excited about?' she inquired coldly.

'We're just crossing the coast,' announced Worrals.

'Is there something unusual about it?'

'Er — no.'

'Fine. I thought from your expression that there was. We'd better see about getting ready to hop out, hadn't we?'

'Bill will give us the tip when we're over St. Vance. Just before reaching the French side of the Channel he's going to cut the engines in the hope that we shan't be heard. Ah! There they go,' she went on, as the bellow of the engines died away to a low purr.

Standing up, side by side, the girls looked down. It was now pitch dark, and the earth appeared as a sombre shadow that rolled away, it seemed, to infinity. Across it, tiny grey threads marked the position of roads, and black, irregular-shaped patterns, the woods and forests.

Search-lights probed the darkness. Far to the east a cluster of dull red sparks hung in the sky and marked the position of British bombers that were harassing the Channel ports. Occasionally the whole sky was lighted up by the blazing white light of bursting bombs. But the Havelock was too far away for the sounds of war to be heard.

'I think we're lucky,' observed Worrals. 'There's evidently a raid on over there to the east and the fuss should distract the enemy's attention from us. We must be nearly over our objective, so we'll get ready to step out.'

She looked at Bill, and saw that he was signalling to her. She went forward.

'We're there,' said Bill. 'I'll throttle back as far as I dare to give you a better take-off. So long, kid-and good luck.'

'So long, Bill — see you at midnight.'

Worrals caught Bill's free hand, gave it a firm grip and returned to Frecks.

'Okay,' she said calmly. 'I'll go first. Give me three seconds to get clear, then follow. Don't leave it longer or we shall land miles apart and perhaps have a job to find each other. If you don't see me when you get on the floor, hoot like an owl.'

Worrals opened the cabin door and looked down into the void. The machine was still gliding quietly, at little more than stalling speed.

'Stand by,' she said tersely, taking the parachute ring in her right hand. Then, drawing a deep breath, she launched herself into space. She counted one — two — three. . . . and then pulled the ring. A moment later a jerk on her harness told her that the parachute had opened. Above her an enormous black cloud had blossomed out. She appeared to float in space. There was no sensation of falling. Looking up, she saw another black mushroom some distance away, and knew that Frecks, too, was on her way down. She could hear the murmur of the aircraft receding into the distance. Gradually it died away and silence fell, silence utter and complete.

She stared into the void below. The details of the ground became clearer as she sank towards it; roads and woods became easily distinguishable. She could see several villages. One was almost immediately beneath her, and she found herself wondering what would happen if she landed in the middle of the village street. However, she soon saw that this would not happen, and she judged that she would hit the ground about a mile to the west of the field from which she had taken off a few hours earlier. She recognized it by the clump of trees, and the lane that meandered from it to the village.

Still gazing down, a queer sensation crept over her that she was not falling, but was hanging suspended in space. It was a strange feeling. Then, suddenly, the colourless earth seemed to leap towards her, and she bent her knees in readiness for the shock of contact. When it came she sprawled headlong, but was quickly on her feet, groping for the quick-release clip. But the air was still, so there was no danger of being dragged, and the folds of the parachute billowed softly to earth beside her. Moving quickly, she got out of her harness and folded it, with the fabric, into a bundle. Looking round she saw that she had landed in the middle of a field of turnips, or some similar root crop. She couldn't see Frecks, but that didn't surprise her, for a three-second interval between the jumps would be sufficient to carry Frecks a fair distance away. Then came a hoot from the darkness. It bore little resemblance to the sound an owl normally makes, but it served its purpose, and Worrals hurried in the direction from which it came. Soon she saw Frecks, squatting on her bundled parachute hooting mournfully.

'All right, that's enough,' said Worrals, as soon as she was within speaking distance. 'I never heard an owl make a noise like that.'

'Neither did I,' confessed Frecks. 'But then, I'm not an owl.'

'You might put in a bit of practice when we get home, for future occasions,' suggested Worrals. 'Come on, let's get going.'

'Which way?'

'We're less than a mile from the clump of trees where the Reliant landed yesterday,' answered Worrals. 'We'll make for it because, in the first place, we can hide our brollies under the trees — we've got to get rid of them somehow. Secondly, we shall know exactly where we are. We'll take the lane from the leaning signpost to the village.'

Proceeding cautiously, and often stopping to listen, they reached the wood without incident. All was silent. Pushing their way into the undergrowth they thrust the parachutes under a holly bush, and then, after tramping across the field to the lane, set off for the village. It was dark, but there was no fog, so there was little risk of losing the way. They walked in silence, their eyes exploring the road ahead of them.

In this way they made good progress, and soon came within sight of the village. Nobody was about. In fact, everything looked precisely the same as when they had first seen it. With eyes and ears alert they walked down the short, stone-flagged pavement, feeling their way with their feet, for the path was not very even.

'Are you going straight to the church?' asked. Frecks softly.

'No,' answered Worrals. 'I think we owe it to Captain Charles to report our return, and tell him what we propose to do. After all, this is largely his affair. It was he who introduced us to the padre. He himself may be working on an escape plan, and it wouldn't be fair to crash in on it without giving him warning.'

'Where are you going to looking for him?'

'In the *estaminet* — there's nowhere else.'

'Don't forget Joudrier's friend. We don't want to collide with him.'

'I had no intention of entering the *estaminet* by the front door — you may be sure. I was thinking of going quietly to the side entrance and having a peer around the curtain. In that way I ought to be able to survey the room without being seen.'

'Suppose Captain Charles isn't there?'

'We'll deal with that contingency if it arises. I'll tell you what, Frecks. There's no need for us both to go to the *estaminet*. You wait here. I'll have a dekko, and then come back and let you know how things stand.'

While this conversation had been going on the girls had moved forward until they stood in the pitch dark recess of the church entrance, a position from where it would be possible to observe anyone in the street with little likelihood of being noticed. A faint chink of light a little further along marked the position of the *estaminet*.

'Stand fast — I shan't be many minutes,' whispered Worrals, and she had taken a step forward when a door not far away — she couldn't see quite where — opened and closed. Footsteps, approaching, grated on the paving stones.

Worrals was taking no unnecessary chances, and she withdrew instantly to where Frecks was waiting.

'*S-h-h,*' she breathed, 'someone's coming.'

A second later it was revealed that there were at least two pedestrians, both men, for they were talking in low tones. Another moment brought them into view, not half a dozen paces from where the girls were crouching back against the stone wall of the church. All they could see was two silhouettes. At this particular moment neither of the men was talking, but having reached a position precisely in front of the church entrance, as if by mutual consent, they halted.

'We'll wait here,' said one, in a low voice, speaking in German. At the same time he edged a little nearer to the entrance.

For one ghastly moment Worrals thought they were going to enter the church, but it was soon made clear that this was not their intention. They stopped just inside the porch, facing the street.

'We shall be able to watch from here,' said the second man.

Worrals could not see his face. Nor was this

necessary for her to identify the speaker. She knew the voice. She knew it only too well. It was Joudrier.

Worrals' heart stood still. The shock was almost paralysing. For a few seconds she stood petrified, her brain in a whirl, trying to get a grip on the situation. Then, recovering, she moved her hand and gave Frecks a reassuring pat on the arm — an assurance she certainly did not feel. All she could think of at that moment was, Joudrier had escaped after all. As if that were not bad enough, he had arrived at St. Vance, and his presence now threatened the collapse of the rescue plan. He had only to get one glimpse of the girls and that would be the end. Fortunately, he hadn't seen them yet, but her skin went goose flesh at the narrowness of the escape, for had he arrived only a few minutes earlier they must have collided with him. Not that they were out of the wood yet. But at least they had the advantage of knowing that he was in the village, and could take steps accordingly. Meanwhile, Joudrier and his companion had resumed their conversation, and the intensity of the interest with which Worrals listened can be better imagined than described.

'He usually arrives about this time,' said Joudrier's companion.

'Good. We shall be able to see him when he goes in.'

'Why not grab him then?'

'No. Admittedly, we should get the man, but I want them all. I want to know just what is going on here. I don't trust that *curé*. He's in the thing, whatever it is.'

Worrals did not know definitely to whom this conversation referred, but she had a shrewd idea. Clearly the men were Nazi agents, and the 'thing' to which they alluded could only mean the British refugees hidden in the crypt. In this respect Worrals felt that she was better informed than they were. Evidently they suspected that something was going on, but they did not know what it was. They were now watching the *estaminet* in the hope of finding out — at least, that is what Worrals assumed, for the men were looking in that direction. She felt that had they been actually watching the church they would not have stood in the doorway. The question was, for whom were they waiting? She thought she knew the answer. It could only be one man — the little pseudo-French peasant, Captain Charles.

And at that moment, as if in answer to her racing thoughts, he came into sight, humming softly under his breath, hands in his pockets, strolling casually towards the *estaminet*. He passed within a few feet of the church porch, but, to Worrals' unspeakable relief, he did not stop.

He walked on to the *estaminet* and went in. For a fleeting moment his figure was outlined against the glow of light as he opened the door.

'That's our man,' said Joudrier's friend.

'Good. I take it he doesn't know who you are?'

'I don't think so.'

'He doesn't know me at any rate,' said Joudrier. 'Come.'

The two conspirators left the church porch and followed Captain Charles into the tavern.

'Phew,' gasped Frecks. 'I aged ten years in those ten minutes. Those beasts are after Captain Charles. Would you believe that such a thing could happen at this very moment?'

'If I had any sense I should have made allowance for the possibility,' muttered Worrals. 'When you come to think of it, it was pretty obvious that if Joudrier succeeded in getting out of England he would come here. This is where he dropped his message, so we should have foreseen that as he had confederates here he would try to reach them.'

'What are we going to do about it?'

Worrals thought for a moment.

'This upsets our programme,' she decided. 'I'm afraid it's going to be hard to get into touch with Captain Charles while those two Nazis are watching him, and from what they said they're not likely to let him out of their sight.'

'Then why not ignore the *estaminet* and try to get into touch with the padre?'

'If it was a matter of just rescuing the Tommies we might do that, but we can't leave Captain Charles to his fate. He doesn't know he's being watched. Suppose he decides to visit the crypt? That would tell the Germans just what they want to know. It might happen at any moment. We've got to work fast.'

'Doing what?'

'First, we've got to warn Captain Charles. He's no fool. Once he knows he is being watched he'll make his own plans to throw those two Nazis off his trail. I'm going to see what's happening in the *estaminet*. You wait here. I'll be as quick as I can. If anything goes wrong — I mean, if I don't come back — try to get word to the padre. If the worst comes to the worst keep the appointment with Bill and save yourself.'

Without giving Frecks time to reply Worrals began moving silently towards the side entrance of the *estaminet*, no great distance away.

9

Captain Charles is Warned

Worrals walked straight to the side doors of the *estaminet*, for this, she felt, would be less likely to create suspicion, if she were seen, than a furtive approach. Having reached it, she tried the door. It opened, so she went in and closed it behind her. As before, the woodshed and corridor were lighted by asingle dirty electric light bulb, so progress was easy. She went straight on to the inner door, from behind which came the faint murmur of voices and the clink of glasses. In spite of her efforts to steady it, her heart beat faster as she quietly turned the handle and pulled the door open an inch or so, taking care that the curtain was not disturbed. The sounds were, of course, instantly amplified. For a few seconds she listened, but everything appeared to be normal, so taking the edge of the curtain in her hand to keep it steady, she moved it a trifle and peeped into the room.

The scene within was at once photographed on her mind. It was much as she expected to find it. There was the usual sprinkling of men, mostly local labourers. Seated immediately in front of her, at the same table where she had first seen him — evidently his regular position — was Captain Charles. He was reading a newspaper. At a distance of a dozen paces, on the right hand side of the room from Worrals' position, seated at a small round table were Joudrier and his companion. She noticed that they were both placed so that they could watch Captain Charles, although there was no indication that he was aware of this. The same girl was behind the counter. She seemed ill at ease, as though aware something was amiss.

Worrals was now in a quandary. To enter the room without being seen instantly by Joudrier was manifestly impossible. She couldn't hope to attract Captain Charles's attention while he remained in his present position, for his back was towards her; nor was it possible to speak without the words being overheard by customers other than the man for whom they were intended.

Worrals backed away from the curtain to

think the matter over. As far as she could see there was only one way of conveying a message, and that was by writing a note and flicking it on the table at which Captain Charles was sitting. She had been pretty good at flicking notes when she was at school, and while she was by no means certain that she would succeed at the first attempt she thought she had a good chance. She had a pencil but no paper, but this difficulty she overcame by tearing the margin from an old newspaper which she found in the woodshed. It took her only a moment to write:

'Beware. You are watched. Rendezvous as soon as possible at usual place.'

Here Worrals hesitated. She daren't risk using the word 'crypt' in case the message fell into wrong hands. She thought that 'usual place' would be understood if she signed herself 'W.A.A.F.', which she did, after adding to the message:

'You will be followed when you leave, so don't go direct.'

Rolling the slip of paper into a small flat pellet she returned to the curtain. The positions of those in the room remained unchanged.

Balancing the pellet on her thumb nail, she took careful aim and flicked it through the air. To her dismay it missed its mark. It struck the edge of the table and rebounded along the floor towards the counter. Captain Charles moved, as though he had heard a sound, but failed to see the pellet.

But someone else had seen it — the girl behind the counter. She saw it because, as she polished a glass, deep in thought, her eyes happened to be on that particular section of floor along which the pellet rolled. Her eyes focused on it. Then, instinctively, she looked up, to see where it had come from. She saw Worrals who, in her agitation, had allowed rather more of her face to show beyond the edge of the curtain than was discreet. For a fleeting instant their eyes met, and in that instant a message seemed to pass between them. Indeed, the girl made a slight inclination of her head that could only be taken as a nod of understanding. She flashed a glance at the two Germans; then, unhurriedly, she walked round the counter and dropped her glass cloth, as if by accident, over the pellet. When she picked it up the pellet was no longer on the floor. She went on to the table at which Captain Charles sat and collected his empty glass. She didn't speak — at least, if she did, the words were inaudible to Worrals. Nor did Worrals see the note change hands, although she guessed it had.

The girl returned to the bar and went on with her task of washing glasses. She didn't even glance at the curtain. Worrals had by this time withdrawn to a safer position, but one from which she could still see Captain Charles. Watching him closely she saw him unfold the pellet under the newspaper. He read it. Then he put it in his mouth and chewed it.

Worrals took a deep breath of relief. So far so good she thought, and decided to return forthwith to Frecks, who would certainly be getting worried. Closing the door she went swiftly down the passage to the side entrance, where she was brought to an abrupt halt by the sound of voices outside. This was annoying, but she was not unduly alarmed, assuming the conversation to be between two villagers. She wished they had chosen some other spot for their debate. For two or three minutes she waited impatiently for them to move off but when they did not do so she determined to leave anyway. Further delay might mean that Captain Charles might arrive first at the church, and he would certainly not want to tarry there.

It was a natural precaution that she should switch out the electric light before opening the door. Having opened it, a shock awaited her. To her horror and amazement, not one or two, but seven or eight men were there, lined up on the pavement. One who stood a little apart was addressing the others — in German. Worrals could just make out the outlines of German uniforms. Before she could draw back, or even think of escape, the leader had turned sharply towards the door and collided with her. In a flash he had grabbed her by the arm and turned the beam of a torch on her face.

'Who are you?' he demanded harshly, still speaking in German.

Worrals did not lose her head. She answered, in French, that she did not understand.

Upon this the German called forward a man who could speak French, and in this Ianguage he repeated his leader's question.

'I'm the kitchen girl,' answered Worrals.

'She says she's the kitchen girl,' repeated the

trooper.

'Ask her what she's doing here at this time of night.'

The man repeated the question in French.

'I've been working late — I'm just going home,' explained Worrals.

The leader switched out the torch. 'All right, let her go. We've had no orders about women,' he said crisply.

Worrals, released, began to move away. It was a good thing that the torch had been switched out, for a moment later another voice spoke. It was Joudrier's.

'What's going on here?' he asked curtly.

'Only a girl, Hauptmann,' replied the leader of the storm troopers.

'A girl? Where did she come from?'

'From the *estaminet*.'

'I saw no girl.'

'But she came out. It was the kitchen wench.'

'So! Where is she?'

'I let her go, Hauptmann.'

'You are sure it wasn't a man?'

'Quite sure, Hauptmann.'

'What are you doing, standing out here in the open? My orders were that you were to remain under cover until I sent for you.'

'I did not get that order, Hauptmann. I was told to report to you at the *estaminet*, and I was about to do so. We have only just arrived.'

'How did you come?'

'In a lorry, Hauptmann.'

'Where is it?'

'In the square.'

'Very well. Take your men to a position where you can't be seen. On no account show yourselves unless you hear my whistle. That will be the signal that I need assistance, so make for the sound as quickly as you can. I may not need you, but be ready. I just came out to see if you had arrived. Our man is still inside. If he leaves we shall follow... I'm going back in now.'

'*Jawohl,* Hauptmann.' The storm trooper clicked his heels and turned to his men.

Worrals heard every word of this conversation distinctly, for the simple reason that she was standing in a doorway less than a dozen yards away. Anxious as she was to put a safe distance between her and Joudrier she could not resist the temptation to listen to what he had to say. So, although her legs were still weak from shock at the narrowness of her escape, she pressed herself flat into the shadow of the doorway and listened. Her brain was in a whirl, for the arrival of the storm troopers had put a new complexion on the affair, and she wished she could have warned Captain Charles of their presence. Things were not going at all well, she thought, as she hurried on to the church.

'For the love of Mike! Where have you been?' greeted Frecks irritably.

'Not so loud,' whispered Worrals. 'Things are happening. The place is stiff with storm troopers.'

'Then for goodness sake let's get out of it. At any rate, let's get in the crypt.'

Worrals went to the church door, but as she expected, it was locked.

'We can't get in until Captain Charles comes,' she said.

'Knock on the door. It may bring the padre.'

'Not likely. If we start hammering on the door we shall bring half the village along. That won't do. I've arranged for Captain Charles to join us here and it would be folly to depart from that arrangement now.'

'What happened?' asked Frecks.

Briefly, Worrals told her. Frecks was silent for a little while.

'This show isn't turning out as easy as we expected.'

'Shows rarely do,' Worrals pointed out, sadly.

'I can't see how Captain Charles is going to get here without bringing Joudrier and Co. on his trail.'

'Neither can I,' confessed Worrals. 'We shall have to leave that to him. There's nothing we can do about it. He ought to be able to find a way.'

There was a brief silence.

'Well, he doesn't seem to be coming,' muttered Frecks.

'I've just thought of something,' exclaimed Worrals. 'I noticed a fuse box in that woodshed.'

'I'm not interested in fuse boxes,' returned Frecks.

'I am,' declared Worrals. 'I could put out all the lights in the *estaminet*. That would give Captain Charles a chance to get clear.'

'What about the storm troopers?'

'They won't move unless they get orders from Joudrier. It's a chance, and I'm going to take it.'

'Personally, I think you're crazy,' said Frecks. 'Can I come?'

'No. You'll have to stay here in case Captain Charles turns up. If he does, tell him I'll be right back. I shan't be long.'

Even Worrals, as she walked quickly along

the pavement to the *estaminet*, thought that the enterprise had taken a desperate turn; but progress had so far been too slow, and unless something were done to speed matters they would certainly not be able to keep the rendezvous with Bill. Reaching the side door, she glanced up and down the street, but seeing no one she went in. The first thing she noticed was that someone had switched the light on again, but this was all to her advantage, for it enabled her to go straight to the rusty fuse box. She wondered if it was worth risking a peep into the room to make sure that Captain Charles was still there, but on second thoughts she decided that it was not. It was no use being too ambitious. Reaching up to the fuse box she grasped the lever and dragged it down. Instantly, the light went out, and a babble of voices broke out in the bar. However, she did not remain to watch results, but groping her way to the door sped back to the church. Even before she reached it there was a murmur of voices as the people who had been in the *estaminet* poured out into the street. Joudrier's voice could be heard above the others.

'Now you have sent the balloon up', muttered

Frecks.

Before Worrals could answer there was a swift patter of footsteps. A voice said tersely:

'Are you there?'

'Yes,' answered Worrals, recognising Captain Charles's voice. 'We want to get into the crypt.'

'Come this way — quick!'

'But—'

'Don't argue — come.'

Worrals wasted no time in parley, for footsteps, hurrying footsteps, could be heard in several directions. Nudging Frecks she followed Captain Charles down a narrow alley beside the church. It took her all her time to keep pace with him.

'Steady,' she panted once. 'For goodness sake don't lose us or we're sunk.'

Captain Charles opened a small iron gate which gave access to an open area. The watery crescent moon revealed rows of ornate French tombstones.

'It's all right. It's only the churchyard,' whispered Worrals for Frecks' benefit.

'Only!' moaned Frecks.

'Keep going,' ordered Captain Charles, and

hurried on towards the dark silhouette of a large building. 'This is the padre's house,' he explained, as he rapped on the door.

Almost at once there came the sound of bolts being drawn, and a lock turned. Then the door was opened a little way, revealing in the light of a candle the anxious face of the padre. He stepped back when he saw who his visitors were, and as soon as they had entered, relocked the door. Without a word he led the way to a small room furnished as a library.

'What has happened?' he asked quickly.

'I don't know exactly,' answered Captain Charles, looking inquiringly at the girls. 'They warned me that I was being watched.'

'I'd better explain,' volunteered Worrals, noticing that the padre was staring at her — as indeed he had every reason to, considering that when he had last seen her she was on her way to England. 'It's a long story, but I'll give you the main facts,' she went on. 'We're acting on behalf of the Intelligence Service. The Germans know that something is going on here. They're on your trail. Two special agents were in the *estaminet* tonight for the express purpose of watching you, and eventually arresting you. There are also storm troopers in the village. Our express purpose is to transport to England the boys who are hiding in the crypt. We said we'd come back, and here we are.'

'You lost no time,' put in the padre, with a ghost of a smile.

'There was no time to lose,' returned Worrals shortly. 'You would all have been taken into custody tonight. I must warn you, padre, that you are suspect. We have an assignation with a troop-carrying aircraft at twelve midnight, in the field by the leaning signpost. We've got to get the boys there by then. In the circumstances I think you'd both be well advised to come too. If you stay here you'll certainly be arrested.'

Captain Charles nodded.

'I've been waiting for such a chance. Actually, I myself could have left here some time ago, but that would have meant abandoning the boys, or throwing all the responsibility on the padre. Why do they suspect him?'

'I don't know, but it is so — I heard the head spy say so,' replied Worrals. 'You know Nazi methods as well as I do, probably better; once a man is suspect they don't need evidence. It's a short step to the concentration camp. That is why, if he has no particular reason for remaining, the padre should come with us to England. No doubt he could find useful employment in the Free French service.'

Captain Charles looked at the padre.

'What do you say?'

'Make up your mind quickly, Father', put in Worrals. 'Time is short, and we have yet to plan how we are to get to the rendezvous.'

'If you can find room for me I shall be glad to come', decided the padre. 'For some time I have been collecting information likely to be useful to the British, but not daring to commit it to paper I carry it in my head.'

'Then that settles it,' declared Worrals. 'There will be plenty of room in the machine. Our task now is to get ourselves, and the boys, to the field, with the least possible delay. You know the district better than I do, so you'd better take charge of the situation from now on.'

'It would have presented no difficulty in the ordinary way,' put in Captain Charles, 'but as you know things have been rather stirred up in the village. A crowd would certainly attract attention. Let's see, what's the time now?' He glanced at the clock. 'Ten minutes past eleven! We shall certainly have to move fast. First, we'd better go across to the crypt and get the party together. The sooner we let the boys know what's afoot, the better.'

He turned to the padre:

'I think I'd better leave it to you to get us across, in case — '

He broke off short as heavy footsteps could be heard approaching the house. They stopped. An instant later the house echoed to a thunderous hammering on the door.

'I fancy our enemies are on the threshold,' said the padre evenly. 'Only Germans knock like that.'

10

A Terrible Decision

There can be a wide variety of expressions in the way a door is knocked. To Frecks, on the present occasion, it sounded like the knell of doom, and her heart sank. Whatever Worrals may have felt remained her own secret, for she gave no indication of it. Actually, her overwhelming emotion was regret that she should thus have put the good padre's life in jeopardy.

'What would you advise us to do?' she asked calmly, looking at the padre. 'You must, of course, act primarily in your own interest.'

'We may outwit them yet,' returned Father Giraldus. 'This house was built at a time when religious persecution resulted in the introduction of hidden chambers. You may find this one a trifle uncomfortable. I use it as a wine cellar.'

As he spoke he pulled aside a loose square rug that covered the centre part of the floor.

The girls could see no difference between the floorboards thus exposed, but when the padre applied pressure with his hands a section tilted on a pivot disclosing a cavity. A number of cases almost filled it. These he pushed on one side, but even so by the time the girls and Captain Charles had dropped into the chamber there was little room for movement. The light overhead was blotted out as the cover was adjusted and the rug replaced. By this time the knocking on the door had become imperative, and they heard the padre's footsteps recede as he went to answer the summons. Then, for a little while all they could hear was the mutter of voices, too far away for the words to be distinguished. This was followed by the sound of footsteps approaching. Presently they thumped overhead. Those below could hear everything that passed.

'Search the house by all means,' invited Father Giraldus. 'I repeat, you will find nobody.'

'These people were seen to leave the church and come this way.' This was said, in French, by Joudrier. Worrals recognized the voice. It was harsh with anger.

'Surely I can't be held responsible for

unknown people moving about the village,' protested the padre.

'Where could they have gone if they didn't come here?'

'Have you searched the churchyard?'

'Yes.'

'Then I have no suggestion to offer.'

'You are sure they didn't come here?'

'I am certain they couldn't have entered this house without my being aware of it,' replied the padre evasively. There was a brief silence.

'Who are these people, and what is all this about?' resumed the padre naively.

'Do you know a man named Charles Marton? In the village he is known as Captain Charles?'

'Yes, I know him well,' admitted the padre.

'He is an English spy.'

'I hope you are not suggesting that I was aware of this?'

'We don't trust you priests.'

'You have already made that abundantly clear.'

'It will pay you to be civil,' snarled Joudrier.

'Then I had better remain silent,' answered the priest quietly.

'This man who called himself Captain Charles,' went on Joudrier. 'Do you know where he lives?'

'In such a small place, that should be a simple matter to discover.'

'Not so simple as you may think. He comes, and goes, but nobody seems to know where. We are going to find him if we have to tear down every house in the village.'

'With all humility I suggest that that would hardly be a wise procedure.'

'What do you mean?'

'Clearly, there must be someone here, perhaps several people, willing to hide him. As soon as you start tearing down houses it will be known what you are doing. Before you have finished one street he will be miles away.'

Joudrier swore.

'Can you make a better suggestion?'

'Since you ask me, yes. I am only too anxious to see this matter cleared up, because only in that way shall I be able to clear myself of the suspicion which evidently rests on me. Captain Charles will not suppose that he has anything to fear from me. I know every house, and every man and woman in it. I will find him.'

'We will come with you.'

'But that would be fatal. People would soon guess what was going on. It would be much better if you were to wait in the *estaminet*, and allow the excitement of the last hour to die down. I will find Marton. If he refuses to accompany me, as he may, I will let you know where he is to be found.'

There was a brief discussion between Joudrier and his associates.

'Very well, priest,' said the German harshly. 'If you set any value on your life you had better find him, for this I swear. If, by daylight, you haven't found Marton, I will hang you over your own church door.'

'In that case,' returned the padre evenly, 'you may be sure that I shall do my best.'

'What an absolute swine Joudrier must be,' breathed Frecks in Worrals' ear, as the footsteps overhead receded. 'Could you imagine anyone behaving like that?'

'Easily, when you're dealing with Nazis,' answered Worrals drily.

There was silence for some minutes. Then came single footsteps and the trap door was opened.

'I'm afraid I came very near to prevarication,' murmured the padre uneasily. 'All is well — at least for the moment. They have gone to the *estaminet*.'

'You're sure of that?' questioned Worrals.

'I watched them go.'

'I wonder if they have set a guard to watch the house?'

'Wondering will not provide the information,' the padre pointed out. 'That's a risk we must take.'

'Then let us get over to the crypt,' suggested Worrals. 'Unless we move faster than this we're going to be late for our appointment.'

The padre slipped on a black skullcap. 'Let us go,' he said.

'It will mean crossing the churchyard?'

'There is no other way.'

They went to the door, opened it and looked out. The only sound was the rustle of a light breeze in the trees, and the ripple of a nearby brook. Low, heavy clouds were moving slowly across the sky.

'There's going to be a change in the weather,

announced Worrals. 'I don't like the look of those clouds. They mean rain.'

'I'll lead the way,' invited Captain Charles. 'If anyone is watching I shall be seized. In that case you girls would be well advised to remain where you are. Let me have a little start. I'll make for the vestry door. Give me the key, padre.'

Worrals would have preferred that they all went together, but Captain Charles pointed out that the interests of the country would be best served by following his advice. Even if he were captured there would still be a chance of getting the boys home. This, Worrals realized, was true, and she made no further protest.

'If you hear nothing you may take it that all is well — that I have reached the vestry door,' said Captain Charles to the padre, and with that he disappeared into the darkness.

It was an anxious moment, and Frecks could feel her nerves tingling under the strain of waiting. Worrals, tight-lipped, stared into the gloom. Minutes passed.

'Good, he must have got there by now,' whispered the padre. 'That means it's safe for us to go. Keep close behind me.'

As he closed the door and led the way between the gaunt tombs Worrals felt the first splash of rain on her face. She did not give voice to her doubts, but she knew all too well that if the rain persisted it would be folly for Bill to attempt a landing. She could only pray that the squall would pass.

The church appeared, gaunt and stark against the night sky. The padre, of course, knew every stone, and he made straight for the door where Captain Charles was waiting. It was already open. They went in. Again to Worrals' nostrils came the well-remembered musty odour. The padre now took the lead, switching on a pocket torch to light the way. Another minute and they were on the steps leading into the crypt.

Frecks drew a deep breath of relief.

'Phew! That's better,' she whispered. 'I was beginning to feel limp.'

The smell of an oil lamp came up the steps to meet them, and then they were in the centre of an excited group of Tommies, all asking questions at once. It seemed that they remembered Worrals, and her promise of rescue.

'Are we really going?' they clamoured.

'Are we going tonight?' cried one, whose arm was bandaged.

'Did Tim get home all right?' asked one of the airmen.

Worrals held up her hands. 'Quiet, boys,' she ordered. Then, to Captain Charles: 'What's the time?'

Captain Charles looked at his watch. 'Eleven-forty.'

'Then we've got to do everything in twenty minutes,' said Worrals grimly. 'Listen, boys,' she went on quickly, 'this is the position. A troop-carrying aircraft is due to meet us at a field about a mile from here in exactly twenty minutes. If I'm not there to give the signal it won't land. I allowed myself — as I thought — plenty of time, but unfortunately complications have delayed me. However, I think we are now ready to proceed. Those of you who have any kit get it together. We're moving off right away. I want everyone to obey orders to the letter. Absolute silence is essential. Any man who speaks out of turn may cost his comrades their lives.'

There was a buzz of excitement.

'Has anyone anything to say?' demanded

Worrals.

'Lead on, McDuff,' came from a brawny high-lander in a kilt — and little else.

Looking round, Worrals missed the padre.

'Where's he gone?' she asked Captain Charles.

'To save time he has gone to the church door to see that all is clear.'

Hardly had the words left his lips when the padre returned, and one glance at his face was enough to tell Worrals that something was amiss. For the first time the old man looked really upset.

'What is it?' asked Worrals sharply.

The padre threw up his hands.

'A terrible thing has happened,' he lamented. 'They've arrested Suzette.'

'Suzette — who's that?' demanded Worrals tersely.

'The girl at the *estaminet*.'

'How did you learn this?'

'When I got to the door two men were sheltering from the rain in the porch. I overheard their conversation.'

The padre turned to Captain Charles. 'It was on account of a message bag. Do you know anything about it?'

Captain Charles shook his head wearily.

'Silly, silly girl,' he muttered sadly. 'Still, perhaps it was my fault. Yet how was I to know. . . .' He looked at Worrals. 'You may as well know the facts,' he said. 'You remember this man Joudrier dropping a message?'

'Of course.'

'I guessed it was something important, so I decided to get it. As a matter of fact Suzette, who knows who I am and has often helped me, actually took the bag from the coat pocket of the German officer to whom it was given. As I thought, it was a most important document. I have it. Suzette must have failed to destroy the streamer. Naturally, I assumed that she would dispose of such an incriminating piece of evidence, but apparently she didn't. Joudrier, by accident or design, must have got hold of it. He probably searched the house.'

'Is this going to be a serious matter for Suzette?' asked Worrals, although she knew what the answer would be.

'They'll shoot her. The Nazis shoot anybody on the merest suspicion of espionage or sabotage,' answered Captain Charles bitterly. 'If I escape, Joudrier will certainly have his revenge on her. Poor girl. I'm afraid I shan't be able to come after all.'

'Why not?'

'What sort of a man would I be to run away leaving the girl to her fate — after she has helped me?'

'She helped me, too,' said Worrals pensively.

'You go on — you're late as it is,' rapped out Captain Charles. 'I'll do my best to get her away.'

'You haven't a hope you know that,' asserted Worrals. 'You'll both lose your lives.'

She turned to the padre.

'Where is Suzette now?'

'In the *estaminet*, where Joudrier and his accomplice are waiting for me. They have cleared everyone else out.'

Worrals looked round the circle of anxious faces. A terrible decision now rested on her shoulders. Would her conscience allow her to go, leaving Suzette in the hands of her brutal captors? On the other hand, was she justified in risking all their lives for the sake of one person? Her heartstrings seemed to tighten as she made up her mind.

'Boys,' she said, 'you've heard everything. What do you say? We're all in this together. My vote is that we all go, including Suzette, or we all stay.'

There was a chorus of assent.

'Then it now rests on you, padre,' said Worrals.

'On me?' The padre looked surprised.

'Yes, as far as I can see we've one chance left, one hope of getting Suzette. It depends on the success of two missions. I doubt if even now we could get to the field by midnight. The position, therefore, is already desperate — only desperate measures can save us.'

'What do you want me to do?' asked the padre.

'We've got to get Suzette here.'

'But that's impossible!'

'I think not. I want you to go to the *estaminet*. It will occasion no surprise because Joudrier is expecting you. You will adopt a secretive air, and tell him that if he cares to come with you, you can show him the man he is looking for. Unless I've made a mistake he will be only too anxious to accompany you. I can't imagine that he will leave

Suzette in the *estaminet*. He will bring his friend, and Suzette, with him.'

'You mean — bring them here?' cried the padre in credulously.

'That's just what I do mean.'

'But even if we get Suzette, what are you going to do with the two men?'

Worrals showed her teeth in a mirthless smile. 'We've a dozen stout lads here. They should be capable of taking care of a couple of Nazis.'

'You mean — kill them?'

'Certainly not. They're both wanted in England, for espionage. We'll take them back with us. That will just complete the party. Now, padre, it's up to you. Will you do it?'

'Of course.'

'Go to the *estaminet*. Bring them to the front door of the church. We shall be waiting.'

'It's nearly ten minutes to twelve,' put in Captain Charles. 'It will take the padre at least five minutes, even if things go well, to complete his mission. That leaves five minutes to get to the field. How do you propose to do that?'

'That's where I come in,' returned Worrals. 'But do one thing at a time. Get going, padre.

Seconds count now.'

The padre departed.

Worrals turned to the others. 'Now, this is what I want you to do,' she said crisply. 'Take up positions just inside the door. Not a sound, or you'll give the game away. As soon as the padre and the others are inside we spring the trap. I shall switch a light on them. That will be your signal to rush. Have jackets ready to put over their heads, in case they shout. One of them has a whistle. He mustn't be allowed to use it or we shall have a squad of storm troopers to deal with. Frecks, your job will be to close the door as soon as they are inside, then no sound will reach the street. You boys tie the men's hands behind their backs. Use your lanyards. Now let's get into position.'

The highlander spat on his hands and rubbed them together.

'Gosh,' he breathed. 'I've waited six months for this.'

11

Challenge to Storm Troopers

It did not take Worrals long to get the boys into position. Frecks stood behind the open door ready to close it the moment the spies walked into the trap. Captain Charles stood near her in case she needed help. 'Quiet now, everybody,' ordered Worrals, and silence fell.

A ghost of a smile played round her lips as she stood there in the darkness. Nothing could be seen. It was hard to believe that within striking distance the boys were waiting, with muscles tense, for the enemy. She remembered Drake laying his ambush of Devon lads on the Isthmus of Panama, to trap the Spanish Dons with their looted gold. Drake would have enjoyed the present situation, she thought, as she crept to the door and peeped down the deserted street.

Frecks was far from happy. The tension was terrific. Every nerve in her body was strained to breaking point. Waiting is usually a more trying business than action.

Worrals' voice floated back into the darkness like a sigh.

'They're coming!'

With her thumb on the button of the torch she stood ready. Footsteps approached, firm decisive footsteps that said as plainly as words that the walkers had no thought of danger. They turned in the porch, and moved on, slowly now, into the building. Just inside they halted, Joudrier spoke.

'Show a light,' he said harshly.

'Certainly,' answered Worrals, and switched on her torch. 'Get 'em boys,' she snapped. 'The door, Frecks — quick.'

There was a swift rush, a grunt, a strangled cry. The heavy old door thudded into its frame with a dull boom. Worrals kept her torch on, but for a few seconds it was not easy to see what was happening. All that the light revealed was a heap of struggling bodies. Worrals saw that Suzette had also been caught in the rush and was on the floor with the rest, so she made haste to pull her clear.

The French girl was muttering incoherently, obviously unaware of what was really happening. The padre took charge of her while Worrals returned to the scrum.

'Steady there, boys!' she cried. 'Don't kill them.'

Slowly, with gasps and chuckles, the heap of bodies broke into its component parts, and Worrals saw that the boys had done their work well. The two spies, with their arms tied to their sides and with tunics wrapped round their heads, were dragged to their feet. One of the boys handed Worrals Joudrier's whistle. She kept it in her hand.

'Nice work,' she said. 'Stand fast everybody — and don't lose those prisoners. What's the time, Captain Charles?'

'Six minutes to twelve.'

'We're doing fine,' declared Worrals.

'We can't walk to the field in less than a quarter of an hour,' remarked the padre anxiously.

'I realize that,' answered Worrals. 'In that case we shall have to ride. I'm going to fetch a conveyance. If I'm not back in five minutes you will know that I've failed, in which case you had better remain in the crypt and try to keep the rendezvous tomorrow night. Don't wait for me. But I shall, I hope, be back.'

'Where are you going?' asked Frecks in an amazed voice.

'To fetch the lorry.'

'What lorry?'

'The one the storm troopers came in. It's parked in the square.'

Dead silence followed this announcement. Worrals moved swiftly to the door.

'When I come I shall probably be in a hurry,' she said quietly, 'so stand ready to jump aboard.' And with that she stepped out into the still silent street.

She knew exactly what she was going to do, basing her plan on the strict adherence of the storm troopers to their orders. Knowing German methods she had no doubt that they would obey their orders to the letter.

First, she hurried to the square, to confirm that the lorry was still there. It was. But she knew that, although she could not see them, somewhere close at hand were the storm troopers. She did not want them too near the lorry, or when the engine was started they might return to it in time to prevent her from getting away; so she went straight on across the square, and continued on for perhaps a hundred yards. Then, taking a side alley, she explored it quickly and found, as she hoped and expected, that it emerged into another street which terminated — as is usual in French villages — in the public square. Raising the whistle to her lips she sent a shrill blast echoing through the silent streets. Again and again she blew, short, sharp blasts.

She had not long to wait for the result. The village seemed to come to life. The street resounded with the thud of running feet. Men shouted to each other as they ran. One more blast Worrals blew; then, flinging the whistle from her, she darted back down the alley, and turning up the main street raced for the square.

She had a nasty shock when she nearly collided with a storm trooper, for the others, as she intended, had run down the street in which she had blown the whistle. The man saw her at once, and switched the torch on her face.

Worrals kept her head. Pointing down the street she cried:

'They're down there!'

The man, seeing only a girl, and not having the imagination to associate her with the uproar ran on towards the scene of the supposed disturbance. Worrals tore on to the square, but there another shock awaited her. The lorry was still in the same place, but the driver, who when she had last seen the vehicle must have been in his seat, was standing by the running board. Curiously enough Worrals was not in the least flustered. A strange calm had come over her. Her brain worked as easily and smoothly as a well-oiled machine. She ran straight over to the man.

'Quick,' she gasped, speaking in German. 'Your chief is being murdered. There is fighting. Everyone is wanted.'

But the man was not so easily hoodwinked — or at any rate, he did not react as Worrals thought he might. She hoped, of course, that he would run straight down the street after the others. Instead, to her horror, he jumped up into his seat, evidently with the intention of driving to the spot Worrals had indicated. He didn't even trouble to shut the door. Before she could think of an alternative plan he had started the engine.

'Let me come with you,' pleaded Worrals, and without waiting for an answer sprang up into the spare seat. The vehicle was now moving slowly.

'Get off!' shouted the man as the car gained speed.

Worrals raised both her feet, and using all her strength, kicked swiftly and viciously.

The man, taken completely by surprise, was jerked out of his seat. He made a wild clutch at the swinging door, missed it, and thumped to the ground. At any rate, he disappeared, and Worrals

wasted no time looking to see what had happened to him. She slipped into the driving seat and swung the wheel hard over just in time to avoid collision with a house. The lorry did, in fact, hit a telegraph pole, and the pole went over with a crash that did nothing to calm Worrals' now agitated state of mind. The crash was followed by a shot, and a bullet ripped a splinter of wood from the bodywork unpleasantly close to her head.

But by this time she had the lorry under control. She settled herself in the seat, got one foot on the accelerator and the other on the brake, and took a firm grip of the wheel. She could have shouted with joy as the thought flashed into her head: 'I've got it.'

She couldn't see what was happening behind her, but she could form a pretty good idea. There were more shots, but none came as close as the first one. Still, she realized that by this time the whole pack of storm troopers, hearing the shots, would be making back for the square, and would soon be on her trail. She prayed that the boys might be ready when she got to the church, now less than fifty yards away. To make sure she hooted the horn in a series of staccato blasts.

What with the shots, the rumble of wheels on the rough road, and the horn, the din, after the deadly silence, was terrific. The scream of brakes, as Worrals brought the lorry to a skidding stand-still outside the church, only added to it.

'Come on!' she yelled without leaving her seat. She realized that quiet tactics could not longer serve any useful purpose. It was every-thing or nothing, now. Figures poured out of the church, and made for the lorry.

'Get in anywhere!' shouted Worrals. 'Padre, come and sit with me, to make sure I don't take the wrong road. What's the time?'

'One minute to twelve.'

'Okay. Captain Charles, yell when everyone is aboard.'

The men were getting into the back of the vehicle, so Worrals, of course, could not see them.

'Right away!' shouted Captain Charles.

'Got the prisoners?'

'Yes.'

Worrals released the brake and put her foot on the accelerator. The truck leaped forward just as a fusillade of shots crashed out somewhere behind. They ricocheted, screaming, between the houses. Madness seemed to come upon Worrals. She laughed hilariously. No doubt it was reaction, following the strain of the last few minutes.

'Steady!' cried the padre in alarm.

Worrals pulled herself together, realizing that she was driving too fast for safety. It would be silly, she reasoned, to take risks just when success was in sight. One minute, more or less, would make no vital difference. Bill would be bound to give them a few minutes' grace. The storm troopers would be able to judge roughly the direction taken by the lorry by the sound it made, but even so it would take them a good ten minutes to reach the field.

The lorry tore on into the darkness. One thing that pleased Worrals was the weather. The air was still heavy with moisture, and the wheels of the lorry often splashed through deep puddles, but the rain had stopped, and frequent breaks in the clouds allowed the narrow moon, and the stars, to give a little light.

'You're coming to the lane — on the right,' shouted the padre, and Worrals swung the lorry into it. For the first time in her life she found herself driving a vehicle the welfare of which concerned her not a scrap. As long as it held together for another minute — that was all she cared. She could have laughed as it bumped and jolted over potholes. The leaning signpost loomed up, and she stopped with a jerk. In a moment she was standing on the road, staring up into the sombre sky, her red torch held ready in her hand.

'Get the boys out,' she told Frecks, who had made haste to join her. Then she listened — and heard the sound that she had prayed she might hear. It was the drone of a heavy bomber some-where overhead, although precisely where was not easy to determine. Holding up the torch she sent the pre-arranged signal, and repeated it. Almost immediately the drone of the engines died away, and she knew that Bill had seen it. He had cut his engines and was gliding down.

One thought perturbed her. The aircraft, as was only to be expected, was still at a consider-able height; she could tell that from the sound of the engines. It would take Bill several minutes to get down. Would he be in time? Naturally, not knowing the desperate urgency of the situation, he would not hurry.

'Keep together, boys,' she ordered. 'Take care

of the prisoners. Frecks, go down the lane a little way and keep cave. If you hear anyone coming report back to me at the double.' To Captain Charles and the padre she said: 'It looks like being a close thing if the storm troopers follow our trail. It will take the aircraft a few minutes to get down.'

But now that the crucial moment had arrived, Worrals' fear was not so much that they might be overtaken as that Bill might make a bad landing in the dark. Without any boundary lights, or flare track, this was more than possible. Indeed, in her anxious state of mind it seemed highly probable. Then she went cold all over as a new sound came from the indigo dome overhead. It was the snarling grunt of machine-gun fire, and she knew it could only mean one thing: Bill was being attacked by a night fighter. The thought appalled her. She daren't contemplate it. It was about time, she thought bitterly, that they had a bit of luck for a change. Nothing had really gone smoothly. She stared upwards. There were several more bursts of machine-gun fire, but she could see nothing.

Presently to her ears came a different sound.

It was the crescendo whine of a machine diving steeply. All sorts of dire possibilities occurred to her, but she forced herself to remain calm.

Frecks ran up.

'I can hear people coming in the distance — I think they're in the lane,' she announced breathlessly.

'Okay — stand by.' Worrals turned to the boys. 'Any of you fellows got weapons?'

There were, it transpired, two automatic pistols in the party — those that had been taken from the prisoners.

'I hope it won't come to shooting, but it's neck or nothing now so there is a chance that it may,' said Worrals firmly. 'Let the two best shots have the pistols and guard our rear.'

There was nothing more she could do. They could only wait, but the suspense was almost unbearable.

'Hark!' gasped Frecks.

The whine overhead had risen suddenly to the dreadful scream of an aircraft out of control, a sound which once heard is never forgotten. Every face was turned upwards. Some of the boys crouched. Some looked quickly for cover, for as yet there was no indication of where the machine would crash.

'Lie flat, everybody,' ordered Worrals in a dull voice.

Something seemed to have died inside her. Her mouth went dry and she bit her lip to restrain a cry of horror. She forgot to lie down, and it was the padre who reminded her.

'Down!' he cried hoarsely, for it was now certain that if the aircraft did not crash on them it would strike the ground not far away.

With a roar like an express train with its whistle open a black shape flashed overhead. The few seconds between that moment and the time it struck the ground seemed like an eternity. There came a crash as of a mighty tree falling in undergrowth. Then silence. Worrals buried her face in her hands.

Frecks stood up. She said nothing. There seemed to be nothing to say. The men were muttering among themselves. Clearly, they did not know what to do.

Worrals recovered her composure with an effort, although as far as she was concerned she cared little now what happened.

'Sorry, boys,' she said quietly. 'I did my best. I'm afraid our pilot has been killed. You'd better go back to the crypt.'

Suddenly Frecks caught her by the arm in a grip so fierce that it hurt — but she did not mind.

'Listen,' said Frecks, in a funny little hard voice. 'There's another machine up there.'

'Of course . . .' Worrals stared, feeling weak as a new possibility struck her. Up to that moment she had assumed — why, she did not know — that it was Bill's machine that had crashed. But there had been machine-gun fire. That meant that there must have been two aircraft. There had been a combat. Which of them had fallen?

'That was a single-engined machine that went over us,' declared Frecks.

'Are you sure?'

'No, but now I come to think, I fancy — '

'What's the use of fancying?' cried Worrals in a strangled voice. 'Let's find out.'

She started off across the field towards the wreck, but was stopped by a warning shout from Captain Charles. From somewhere up above had come the sullen mutter of idling engines. An instant later, wheels rumbled heavily on the ground, rumbled and rumbled again. Engines growled.

Worrals sprang up, waving her torch, regardless of who saw it. As if in answer, there came a renewed growling of engines, and a huge black shape materialized out of the darkness.

'It's Bill!' yelled Frecks hysterically. 'Look! It's a Havelock!'

The machine rolled on ponderously to where Worrals was still showing the light. She ran forward and the aircraft came to rest. A head appeared above the cockpit cowling.

'Is that you, Worrals?' It was Bill's voice.

Worrals was so overcome that she could hardly speak, but she managed to gasp: 'Okay, Bill.'

'Get aboard and make it snappy,' called Bill. 'A confounded Hun interceptor trailed me, and we had a little affair. It held me up for a minute or two. Have you got the boys?'

'Yes, they're here,' answered Worrals. 'Come on, boys!' she shouted, and ran to open the cabin door. 'This way.'

It may appear odd, but in the tragic events of the last few minutes she had completely forgotten the storm troopers. Perhaps their proximity seemed a trivial matter compared with — as she thought — the death of Bill. She realized now that it must have been the enemy aircraft that had crashed. Now, in the knowledge that Bill was safely on the ground, she remembered the storm troopers, and looked apprehensively in the direction of the lane.

Instantly her fears were confirmed. A group of men were running towards the spot. She could just make out their dark forms. One of the boys shouted a warning, but it was not necessary, for a weapon flashed and a bullet whistled through the air.

Worrals threw open the cabin door.

'Inside, quickly!' she shouted.

There was a wild scramble to get into the aircraft, but Worrals, like a shepherd counting a flock, remained outside. The padre stood by her while the prisoners were bundled aboard. Suzette followed.

'Where are those boys with the pistols?' asked Worrals viciously.

'We're here, miss,' came the answer.

'Then fire a few rounds to let those Nazis

know that we're armed, and mean business.'

No second invitation was needed, and the pistols spat.

12

Operations Completed

Worrals had no clear recollection of what happened during the next few minutes. As from a distance she heard the padre telling her that all the boys were aboard except the two who were holding the Germans back. She shouted to them to get aboard, pushed the padre in after the men and tumbled in herself. Closing the door she ran through to the cockpit.

'We're all in,' she told Bill crisply. 'Get off as fast as you can — there's a bunch of Huns pretty close — '

'You're telling me,' muttered Bill, grabbing the throttle, as a bullet struck one of the engines.

Worrals dropped into the seat beside him as the engines bellowed and the big machine started to turn. Looking through the side window she saw to her horror that some of the storm troopers had almost reached the aircraft.

One was in the act of raising a sub-machine gun, at a range from which it would be impossible to miss. Instinctively she shrank back from the hail of death that was imminent.

'Look out, Bill!' she cried, and even as she spoke a machine gun started its staccato tattoo. The sound made her flinch, as from a blow, yet in a dazed sort of way she wondered how the bullets had so far missed the cockpit. Bill was sitting bolt upright, one hand on the throttle, the other on the control column, looking through the windscreen as though nothing unusual was happening.

'That sounds like Tim,' he chuckled, without turning his eyes.

'Tim?'

'Yes. That wasn't the Germans shooting — it was Tim. He's an old hand. He waited for the enemy to come right up burning ammunition.'

Worrals stared.

'You mean Tim is in this machine?'

'You bet he is. He offered his services to me as a gunner, and thinking he might be useful, I accepted. Naturally, he was interested in getting his pals away.'

Worrals glanced out of the window and saw the storm troopers retiring. But not all of them. Some lay still on the ground.

'Here we go,' said Bill, bringing the machine in line with the open field. The roar of the engines rose to a vibrant crescendo, and the machine moved forward with swiftly gathering speed. Once or twice the wheels bumped on the uneven ground; then the vibration ceased and the aircraft rose into the air.

Worrals allowed her pent-up breath to escape with a gasp of relief. Her whole body seemed to relax.

'My goodness,' she said weakly, 'that was a bit too hot. I'm afraid I'm no soldier.'

'I've never met a soldier yet who wouldn't have got het up at that moment,' returned Bill. 'It certainly was red hot. Keep your eyes open for enemy aircraft; there are some about — but not so many as there were. Tim has got a brace — one as we crossed the coast and the other right over the rendezvous.'

'We heard it crash. I thought it was you.'

'Yes — naturally. . . Funny, I never thought of that. As a matter of fact, I was only thinking of getting down. I shall try to get Tim as a regular gunner.'

After that, nothing more was said for a while. Worrals was content to sit still and say nothing, for her nerves were still quivering from reaction. For the first time she realized what a strain the last hour had been.

'Bite on some of these,' murmured Bill, pulling a small bag from a pigeon hole in the instrument board and pouring some raisins into her hand. Worrals munched the dried fruit with relish, her eyes on the lowering sky. Once she glanced through the front windscreen and saw the questing beams of searchlights. Some distance away flak sparkled menacingly.

'They're not shooting at us,' observed Bill, guessing her thoughts. 'Quite a lot of our boys are busy tonight, warming up the invasion ports again. With luck we might slip through the barrage without being spotted.'

As it happened, this optimism was not justified by events, for although he turned in a wide circle and climbed up to a great height before putting his nose down and racing across the danger area, the flak found them, and the sky was soon alive with flame and hurtling metal. Then the black carpet that was France faded away behind as they stood out across the Channel.

'Thank goodness we're safe at last,' said Worrals thankfully.

'Almost,' corrected Bill.

'What do you mean — almost?'

'Well, provided we don't bump into a stray balloon, barge into our own barrage, or collide with a Hun charging home from our side.'

Worrals smiled. She knew that the chance of any of these things happening, while possible, was remote. And so it proved. A quarter of an hour later Bill throttled back and began a long glide towards their base. Frecks came forward.

'And what do you want?' inquired Bill.

'Nothing — I'm just a chaperone,' murmured Frecks.

A strange sound now mingled with the drone of the idling engines. Worrals opened her eyes wide, and asked what it was.

'Only the boys, singing,' returned Frecks. 'They seem pleased to be home.'

'I can understand that — so am I,' declared Worrals, as Bill flattened out and the big machine glided up the flare path to a safe landing. A minute later, after taxiing in, he switched off.

'Well, here we are,' he announced.

'Much obliged,' said Worrals.

'See you later,' murmured Bill. 'I've got to put this pantechnicon away. I expect there'll be quite a crowd on the tarmac.'

There was. The entire squadron appeared to have turned out, and a little cheer went up as the refugees stepped out.

Worrals found the C.O. in earnest conversation with an Air Ministry official. He seemed to be in a good humour — so much so in fact that he astonished Worrals by clapping her on the back.

'Good show, Worrals,' he said enthusiastically. 'You girls will be winning the war without us if we don't watch it.'

'I've brought a couple of prisoners back, sir,' announced Worrals. 'What shall I do with them?'

'Prisoners?'

'Yes, sir. Joudrier and his assistant. I think the Intelligence people want a few words with them.'

'Well I'm — ' The C.O. coughed just in time. He shouted to the station sergeant major to muster an escort. The prisoners were led away. Worrals never saw them again. She went over to Suzette who was chattering volubly in her excitement. The rescued troops were taken to the canteen, which had been specially opened for the occasion. A few minutes later all those who had been engaged in the operation were in the C.O.'s office, making preliminary reports to the Intelligence officer. It was all one thing, and that was a deadly tiredness. The M.O., who was there, noticed it, and after speaking to the C.O. told them to go to bed, a suggestion about which Worrals did not argue. Bill had arrived, and he saw them to their quarters, taking Suzette with them. As they walked across the square the sound of cheering came from the canteen. The sergeant-major overtook them. He, too, seemed to be in a better humour than usual.

'I thought you'd like to know that the boys are calling for three cheers for the rescue party', he explained.

'What happened to the padre and Captain Charles?' asked Worrals.

'They're with the boys. I should say they're going to make a night of it.'

'Tell them I'll see them in the morning,' said Worrals, and walked on. At the moment she had only one idea, and that was sleep. 'I feel as though I'd been up for a week,' she told Bill.

At the girls' quarters he had to leave them.

'Good night, kids,' he said affectionately.

Frecks, arm in arm with Suzette, walked on. Just inside the door she turned.

'Worrals,' she said sternly, 'what are you doing?'

Worrals looked up.

'Bill was just helping me off with my mackintosh, that's all,' she explained.

Frecks shook a warning finger.

'What you were doing is not scheduled in the night's operations,' she remarked sarcastically.

'Nor were a lot of other things,' returned Worrals.

The echo of Bill's laugh came out of the darkness.

人人人

And that, really, is the end of the story — at least, as far as the girls were concerned, apart from the official inquiry into the whole affair and the lengthy reports that hid to be completed. At the inquiry, which was attended by Major Gray, Joudrier's friend (who turned out to be a notorious German agent) in the hope of saving himself told everything he knew. This convicted Joudrier, who was not a Belgian at all, but a German who had lived for years on the Belgian frontier, where he had been a customs officer. Provided by the enemy with false papers, he had managed to get into the R.A.F. as a 'free' Belgian. Using the ice cream factory to mask its activities, the warehouse had been the headquarters of the spy ring, although the Green Parrot Dance Hall was often used as a rendezvous. All the spies had been captured in the round-up, but Joudrier and his friend would certainly have escaped had it not been for so small a thing as a geranium leaf, which had set Worrals on the trail. And the geranium leaf would not have been on Joudrie,'s wheel had he not, on the afternoon when he was missing, flown to Gestapo Headquarters at Vichy with a special report. So much Major Gray told Worrals, but what eventually became of the spies she never heard, for the British government is often silent about such things.

The man who called himself Captain Charles was not, it transpired, an official British agent. He was an English author who happened to be living in St. Vance when the French collapse occurred; being able to speak the language fluently he had taken upon himself the task of doing every-thing in his power to hinder the enemy. This had included setting up an organization for the purpose of helping British Tommies to escape, or at any rate find refuge from the Gestapo agents who swarmed over the stricken country. In this he had been helped by some of his local French friends, chief among whom were the padre and Suzette.

The authorities, as soon as they were satis-fied with their credentials, found them work, and Suzette was soon serving in a Free French canteen. Father Girardus was given a commission as a padre in the same service. Captain Charles had no difficulty in getting into the British Intelligence Service. So, with one thing and another, the girls felt that in addition to bringing confusion on certain of the King's enemies, they had helped to make several people happy.

This was proved when, during the following weeks, tokens of gratitude were received. The rescued boys clubbed together and presented the girls each with a gold identity disc with an appropriate inscription on the back. Father Giraldus sent two beautifully bound books. Captain Charles sent an enormous box of chocolates, and Suzette, a parcel of fine lawn handkerchiefs exquisitely embroidered by herself. But the crowning satisfaction came in the form of a sheet of paper, a letter from the Air Council, forwarded through the Commandant of the W.A.A.F., informing them that they had been commended for their courage, skill, and devotion to duty. Bill was awarded the D.F.C. for his part in the operation.

'Looking at all these things,' remarked Worrals, 'it rather looks as if our little effort was appreciated — what say you, Frecks?'

Frecks could only nod enthusiastically. Her mouth was full of chocolate.